THE MYSTERY
AT
COMANCHE CANYON

Book Two

THE MYSTERY AT COMANCHE CANYON

The Misadventures Of Inspector Moustachio

by Wayne Madsen

illustrated by Lisa Falzon

PUBLISHED BY

Community PRESS

VIRGINIA BEACH
VIRGINIA

Published By
COMMUNITY PRESS
239 Windbrooke Lane
Virginia Beach, VA 23462

Library Of Congress Control Number: 2007939238
ISBN 9780979087882

Printed In The United States Of America
12 11 10 09 08   10 9 8 7 6 5 4 3 2 1

2008 First Edition

Visit our website at www.communitypresshome.com

The universe is filled with
endless possibilities just
waiting to be discovered!

CONTENTS

1
The Tallest Of Tales

3
Out Of Toilet Paper

18
A Surprise Guest

29
The Auction

40
Bull's Eye

47
Up The River

54
Two Old Goats

62
Little Magnolia

70
Popcorn Trouble

81
Culprit Confusion

89
If The Tiara Fits

100

The Great Escape

110

Cat Food To The Rescue

120

That's The Ticket

130

I Knew It

139

Cownapper

152

Comanche Canyon

158

The Battle With The Baron

167

Follow The Map

175

The Treasure

184

The Mystery Unraveled

204

Dad's Barbeque

How The Misadventures Began...

On Jake Moustachio's eleventh birthday, his grandmother gave him a very special, magical magnifying glass that had once belonged to his beloved grandfather, the great Inspector Buck Moustachio. Being a would-be detective himself, Jake, accompanied by his eight-year-old sister, Alexa, immediately took the magnifying glass and combed their house for clues in an attempt to solve their first mystery: the whereabouts of their missing cat, Rex. When the two sleuths finally ended their search in the Moustachio's attic, they found their pesky pet and a whole lot more than they bargained for!

To their amazement, they were unexpectedly contacted through the magnifying glass by Delbert, The Keeper of Time, and the children and their cat soon realized that their grandpa's seemingly ordinary magnifying glass was the portal to a world of fantastic misadventures and mysteries to be solved.

Delbert, it seemed, was in desperate need of their help to solve a baffling case. A magical bell that controls all time had been stolen!

With a little help from their new friend, Jake and Alexa were able to figure out how to travel through the magnifying glass and were quickly transported to The Museum of Time, a strange and spooky castle once owned by the famous archaeologist Lord Grimthorpe.

To find out who snatched The Bell of Time, Jake, Alexa, and their crazy cat, Rex, were able to use their keen detective skills to gather clues, while encountering a collection of strange suspects and curious talking animals.

After successfully solving the case, Jake discovered that he is the descendant of a long line of famous detectives and that he is next in line to control the magnifying glass and all its mystical powers. But young Jake Moustachio must be very careful because he also learned that there is another magnifying glass in the universe just like his. Unfortunately, the evil Baron Von Snodgrass possesses it!

Jake is warned that the maniacal Snodgrass will stop at nothing to have both magnifying glasses. The one that is purest of heart and of thought who comes to possess both magnifying glasses will be able to unlock all the mysteries of the universe!

And that—Jake had been told—is him!

Inspector Moustachio is his name, and solving mysteries is his specialty!

And now get ready to read the next thrilling installment in
The Misadventures of Inspector Moustachio:

THE MYSTERY
AT
COMANCHE CANYON

CHAPTER ONE
The Tallest Of Tales

"Lexy, hurry up!" called Jake from the bottom of the staircase. The Moustachios were having a barbecue, and the house was in a buzz of anticipation of the soon-to-be-arriving guests.

"I'm coming, Jake!" Alexa replied, approaching the stairs as she twisted a pink ribbon into her strawberry blond hair. "What's your rush?"

"Grandma Moustachio's in the kitchen with custard-filled cream puffs covered in powdered sugar," explained Jake, licking his lips as he thought about the sweet treats.

"Oh, boy!" exclaimed Alexa. "I love cream puffs almost as much as I love spareribs."

"Well, today is your lucky day because I think we're going to get to gobble them both up!" declared Jake.

Jake and Alexa ran as fast as they could to the kitchen to greet Grandma Moustachio, who was busy cooking the most delicious food for the party.

"Wow!" she said, almost dropping a plate full of hot dogs as the children came running by. "What's the hurry, you two?"

Alexa picked up a handful of hairpins that had fallen out of Grandma's wild-looking, salt and pepper hair, and as she handed them back, she asked, "May we have some cream puffs? Please? Please?"

"Yeah, Grandma," pleaded Jake bouncing all around the kitchen. "Can we?"

1

"Well, I don't know," she thought. "It's getting very close to lunch time."

Jake and Alexa just stood there with big smiles on their faces like two little puppies waiting for a bone.

"O.K.," said Grandma, "but we'll have to hurry. Your parents will be back from the supermarket any minute, and I don't want to get into any trouble!"

"Awesome!" yelled Jake as he and Alexa sat down at the kitchen table.

Grandma Moustachio very precisely undid the wrapping from the tall mountain of cream puffs and very carefully slipped out two. As she was about to rewrap them, she felt a nudge by her foot. She looked down and saw Rex rolling around on the floor, licking his lips.

"*Meow*," he begged.

"Not you, too!" moaned Grandma annoyingly. "I won't have anything left for your guests if you eat all the cream puffs now!"

Rex continued to roll shamelessly all over the floor begging for a cream puff.

"Oh, all right! You can have one, too," she said as she grabbed another cream puff from the tray and placed it in his Critter Detective cat food dish. Rex feverishly gobbled up every bit of his cream puff. Custard filling covered his whiskers from ear to ear. Grandma carefully adjusted her mountain of cream puffs so no one would ever know she removed three and then rewrapped them using a hairpin to fasten the plastic wrap just so.

"I think you're going to need some milk to wash those down with," she suggested, placing the cream puffs on the table.

"Chocolate, please," said Jake.

2

"Make mine strawberry, Grandma," exclaimed Alexa. "You know pink is my signature color. I love all things pink: pink ribbons, pink clothes, pink nails, and, especially, strawberry milk from pink cows!"

Jake crinkled his nose and raised his left eyebrow in exasperation, "Strawberry milk doesn't come from pink cows!" he explained.

"Says who?" snapped Alexa, crinkling her nose back at him.

"Says everybody," snapped back Jake. "There's no such thing as pink cows!"

"Yes there is—"answered Alexa. "Strawberry milk comes from pink cows, chocolate milk comes from brown cows, and white milk comes from white cows."

"That's crazy!" he snickered. "Grandma, help me out here!"

"Oh, no!" she answered, pouring them the last drop of milk. "I know when not to get into the middle of an argument with you two. Your grandpa used to say, '*The most wonderful gift in life is the power to believe.*' You two believe in whatever you want to."

"And I choose to believe in pink cows!" exclaimed Alexa.

"Oh, brother!" frowned Jake.

Grandma had a very perplexed look on her face as she stuck her nose into the refrigerator.

"What's wrong, Grandma?" Alexa questioned, poking her head inside to see what all the fuss was about.

"Why, we're all out of milk!" she announced with a puzzled tone in her voice. "Now, I know your Mom had two gallons in there yesterday. Well—at least I thought she did."

"Maybe the milk bandit stole it!" exclaimed Alexa.

"Or maybe all the white, brown, and pink cows are on vacation!" Jake said with a smirk as he gobbled up the last bit of his cream puff and finished the last drop of his milk. He then proceeded to wipe his face with his sleeve. Through her very thick glasses that always dangled from the tip of her nose, Grandma glared at him in disapproval.

"Jake, use a napkin," she scolded, handing him a pile from the kitchen counter.

As Jake wiped the rest of the custard filling off his face, he noticed some funny writing on the napkin.

"What's that?" questioned Alexa.

Jake held the odd-looking paper up close to his face so he could get a better look. "This isn't a napkin," he remarked as it stuck to his custard covered nose.

Grandma wobbled over to the table and took a look at the funny napkin still dangling from the tip of Jake's nose. "Oh, dear," she uttered, pulling it off. "Why—that's a letter your great-great-grandmother Mary wrote to your great-great-aunt Fay about her barbeque sauce recipe. Well, at least half of it. I never did find out whatever happened to the other half of the letter. This part must have gotten stuck to the pile of napkins when I was going through my recipes for the cream puffs. I never quite got the hang of making her barbeque sauce without those missing ingredients. They must have been written down on the second lost sheet of paper from the letter."

"She had pretty handwriting," said Alexa as she gazed at the flowery dots over Great-Great-Grandma's 'I's.' "

"She was quite a character," recalled Grandma. "She was always telling tall tales about her father and the Wild,

Wild West. In the mid-1800s, her father worked for The Butterfield Overland Mail Route, which was the way the West got their mail back in the old days."

"Old days?" asked Alexa.

"Old days," explained Grandma. "Way before e-mail. Her father was a western mailman, delivering the mail on a horse-drawn wagon, right before the start of the Civil War. One day, according to your great-great-grandmother, her father was traveling along the Red River from Jacksboro when a herd of wild buffalo came stampeding by. His horses became so scared they flipped over the mail wagon, dumping him into a dusty ditch. When he climbed out of the ditch, to his surprise, he stumbled upon an oddly dressed man wearing a colorful buckskin shirt. It was as if the stranger appeared out of nowhere. The man, for some unknown reason, offered to give Great-Great-Grandma's father some cattle that would lead him to a hidden treasure deep within the canyons."

"That's so cool!" yelled Jake.

"All of a sudden, the sunny skies became as dark as night and a horrific dust storm started to blow. The ferocious wind blew the mail all over the canyon spreading it for miles and miles. Being the honorable man he was, he ran around like a jackrabbit gathering up all the letters he could so he could finish his mail route. By the time he collected all the letters and got back to the spot where the peculiar looking man was, he was nowhere to be found."

"What happened to him?" questioned Alexa as she ever-so-daintily wiped the custard filling from her pink, lip-glossed lips.

"He unexplainably disappeared," she answered.

"Hoping to find him, her father drew a sketch on the back of one of his letters so he would remember where to look for the stranger after he finished delivering the rest of his mail."

"Did he ever find him?" asked Jake.

"Nope!" answered Grandma. "The letter with the sketch was supposedly lost and the treasure long forgotten."

"A long-lost treasure!" exclaimed Alexa. "I just love a good mystery."

"This looks like a job for Inspector Moustachio," declared Jake.

"And Inspector Girl!" included Alexa with a proud smile.

"*MEOOOOOOW!*" added Rex, swatting her on the ankle.

"Yes, and you, too, Critter Detective!" Alexa giggled as she scooped him up and gave him a snuggly hug.

"Oh, brother!" groaned Jake, rolling his eyes in annoyance at the spectacle.

"Well, don't get too excited, you three," said Grandma. "That letter was lost a very, very long time ago. I'm not even sure the Red River ever existed, and that tall tale may be just that. Your great-great-grandma had an enormous imagination, but you can always use your own imagination and your power to believe."

As Alexa wiped off the custard from the barbeque recipe, she asked, "Can I keep the recipe, Grandma? I just love the way she wrote her letters. I want to trace them."

"Sure, sweetie," she answered. "I haven't been able to make that barbeque sauce in all these years, anyway. Someday, I hope to find the second missing sheet to the letter with the rest of the recipe on it. Oh, well—go have fun! Though you'd better go wash the custard off your faces before your parents get home, and you might want to clean up Rex, too!"

They all looked down at Rex who was covered from head to toe in custard and powdered sugar.

"*Meooow!*" he burped with delightful satisfaction, rolling all over the kitchen floor, licking up every crumb and drop of custard filling he could find.

"Come on, you messy fur ball, up to the bathroom, and I'll wash you off," scolded Jake.

"And Jake," added Grandma, "you might want to pick up your coin collection from the playroom floor before you lose anything. Every time I see that coin collection, it gets bigger and bigger. Your grandpa and your father started that collection with just three coins—I can't believe how it's grown!"

That reminded Jake about the rare Indian head penny he found earlier that day while playing at the school playground. He stashed it in the front right pocket of his pants, knowing it would be the perfect addition to his collection.

"I will, Grandma," he shouted on his way upstairs, "right after I clean up Rex."

CHAPTER TWO

Out Of Toilet Paper

Rex scooted upstairs with his big, furry, custard-filled belly wobbling back and forth, and followed Jake into the bathroom that adjoined the children's bedrooms. Alexa ran to her overly pink bedroom with the numerous stuffed animals scattered across the bed to get her tracing paper to trace the beautiful handwriting on the letter.

Alexa came into the bathroom just as Jake grabbed Rex's Critter Detective cat brush to groom his messy cat. As he laid down some newspapers on the granite stone floor to catch any falling fur from Rex's coat, Alexa sat down beside them and started tracing the letters with her tracing paper and favorite long-stemmed pink pencil with a pink feathered ball at the end of the eraser. "What's a solar eclipse, Jake?" she asked.

"Why do you ask, Lexy?" he replied.

"It says right here in the newspaper that a total solar eclipse will take place in the western skies today."

Jake grabbed his magnifying glass and read the news story from the paper. "Well, what do you know—" he said. "A total solar eclipse is when the moon moves between the sun and the earth, blocking out the sunlight for a few minutes. According to this article, when the moon covers the last bit of the sun, beams of light reflect off the moon's surface creating an effect called Baily's beads. It looks like a chain of bright, glowing pearls. During this very short part of the eclipse, the Baily's beads have been known to cause people to see things they normally could not see. This type of eclipse hasn't taken place in the western skies for over a hundred years."

"How exciting!" she exclaimed as she tore the article from the newspaper. "I'm going to discuss this during current events at school this week."

"Sounds good to me!" announced Jake as he tugged out a custard-filled fur knot from Rex's golden-red, fluffy belly.

"Don't forget to rub his tummy, Jake, when you're done," said Alexa. "You know how he loves that!"

"How can I forget!" exclaimed Jake. "He practically gave us a list of demands before we left The Museum of Time on our last misadventure."

Alexa giggled remembering the list as she called out Rex's orders, "*Change the cat litter. It smells like roses.*"

"*Tell the housekeeper to stop sucking up my tail when she vacuums under the beds*," continued Jake.

"*Shrimp surprise gives me gas*," Alexa added.

"*And a little tummy rub, now and then!*" they both shouted happily as they rolled all over the floor, giggling with their pesky pal.

"Jake, can I borrow your magnifying glass for a second?" asked Alexa.

"Sure," he said as he took the magnifying glass out of his back pocket. "What do you need it for?"

Squinting in order to see the letters on Great-Great-Grandma's recipe, Alexa replied, "I can't make out this last letter."

"Let me see if I can," said Jake, scanning through the recipe with the magnifying glass.

Jake couldn't make out the last letter either. But as he turned over the recipe, to his amazement he saw through the magnifying glass something else.

"Oh, boy!" he shouted, his big, green eyes widening in delight.

While Rex sniffed the recipe, Alexa inquired, "What do you see, Jake?"

"It's some sort of sketching," he whispered.

"There's no drawing on the back," Alexa pointed out in disbelief.

"Yes, there is!"

"No, there's not!" she replied with determination.

"Look directly into the magnifying glass, Lexy," Jake coaxed.

Alexa and Rex squeezed their faces into the magnifying glass while Jake held the recipe steady. They couldn't believe their eyes. Through the magnifying glass, the blank back of the letter revealed a puzzling sketch.

"This has to be the lost sketch leading back to the spot where Great-Great-Grandma's father met that stranger!" exclaimed Jake.

"*Meow!*" added Rex.

"A missing treasure, Inspector!" whispered Alexa. "We just have to find it! Maybe we can use the magnifying glass to help us!"

"But it looks like only part of a sketch, you guys," Jake observed.

"I'll bet he put the rest of the sketch on the second half of Great-Great-Grandma's letter," suggested Alexa.

"But Grandma said she never found the other half of the letter," Jake added. "Can you imagine if we were somehow able to find that missing part? Put the two letters together and then be lucky enough to find the missing man?"

"Then we could find—*the treasure!*" Alexa exclaimed.

"Well, that's the doggone thing I reckon gotta' do!" yelled an unfamiliar, big, burly voice deep within the magnifying glass.

The children screamed in shock. Startled by the voice, they dropped the recipe and the magnifying glass and jumped into the bathtub with Rex to hide. Rex pulled the shower curtain tightly shut with his trembling paw.

"And we're hiding in the tub because—?" questioned Jake, so red from embarrassment his faced matched his hair.

"*Meooow*," screeched Rex.

Rex pulled the shower curtain open with his paw and poked his head out. Then Alexa poked her head out on top of Rex's, and, finally, Jake poked his head out on top of hers. Jake and Alexa looked like two scoops of strawberry ice cream plopped on top of a golden, furry cone, which was Rex's head. They all stared in awe at the magnifying glass moving up and down on the bathroom floor.

"Delbert did say that after we saved *Time*, we would be called upon to solve many other mysterious cases," announced Alexa.

"We shouldn't be scared. After all, mysteries are our specialty," proclaimed Jake. "Someone may need our help!"

"Or be in grave danger," whispered Alexa.

Rex took a deep breath and slammed shut the shower

curtain with a courageous burst of strength.

The three mystery-solving sleuths formed a circle. Into this circle, Jake put his hand and said, "This looks like a job for Inspector Moustachio. Are you guys in?"

Alexa gave Rex a wink and declared, "Inspector Girl, ready for action!" She then placed her hand on top of Jake's.

Rex placed his right paw on top of Alexa's hand, gave her a wink back, and roared like a lion.

"I'm not sure what that crazy cat just said, but I'll take that as a yes," declared Jake. "**Let's go!**"

They all climbed out of the bathtub. As they got closer and closer to the magnifying glass, they could hear the muffled voice still yelling from the other side.

"Howdy, partner!" shouted the voice. "I reckon you're Inspector Moustachio?"

Jake's hand trembled as he picked up the magnifying glass from the bathroom floor. Wiping away the fog with his sleeve, he could see a big man with a big, black moustache wearing an even bigger black cowboy hat. "I'm Inspector Moustachio," explained Jake. "Yeah—that's right, The Great Inspector Moustachio!"

"And I am the one and only Inspector Girl, and this is our Critter Detective, Rex," announced Alexa. "Who are you?"

"Why I'm Big Daddy—the biggest cow rancher there ever **Waaaaas** and will ever **Beeeee**!" he declared, "and I need all of your help."

"Help with what?" questioned Alexa as she stuck her nose right against the magnifying glass.

"**My doggone cows are—*gone*!**" shouted the voice so loudly it knocked Jake, Alexa, and Rex right back into the bathtub, tearing the shower curtain down over their heads.

"Gone!" muttered Jake annoyingly as he pulled the shower curtain off his head.

"That's what I doggone said—gone," uttered the burly voice.

"Gone where?" questioned Alexa.

"Well, I reckon if I knew that, I wouldn't need to hog tie you three into helping me find them! Now, would I?" scolded Big Daddy.

"Good point!" declared Jake as he crawled out of the tub.

Big Daddy moved closer to the magnifying glass. The children could see only one lonely golden tooth peeking through the fuzziness of his thick black moustache. "Now get a wiggle on," he hollered. "I need you on my side of the magnifying glass faster than a jackrabbit running from a fox. Ya' gotta' solve this caper and get me my doggone cows back from the diabolical rascal who kidnapped them!"

Alexa, in a burst of excitement, ran back to her bedroom shouting, "I need my Inspector Girl backpack. I'll be right back!"

Rex ran to the cabinet below the bathroom sink where Jake's dad kept the extra cat food and rolls and rolls and rolls of extra toilet paper. He feverishly started stacking cat food cans for the trip, one by one until he made a tall pile of ten.

"I don't think so—you nutty fur ball," Jake smirked in disapproval.

Alexa was frantically rummaging through her closet for supplies to fill her backpack. "I said he could take some food on our next case, Jake!" she shouted out from under the rubble.

Rex's big golden eyes had a look of utter despair as he waited for Jake's final decision. He remembered starving through their last misadventure, only to scrounge a morsel of food from Mrs. Smythe, the crazy, cake-poisoning cook at The Museum of Time.

"All right," Jake decided. "Just—one can."

Rex meowed and swatted Jake with his tail in disapproval of his decision.

"Did you just swat me, you pesky ball of hair?" he scolded as he knelt down onto the floor and faced Rex, nose to nose. They glared at each other like two cowboys about to challenge each other in a bronco bust rodeo. Jake removed one can and firmly placed it in his own pile. Rex then removed five cans to another pile as a counter offer to Jake's decision. Jake then added one more can to his pile making it two cans allowed. Rex growled his disapproval while removing one can from his pile and making it four cans to Jake's two.

Jake raised his right eyebrow in utter frustration and exclaimed, "Listen, you pesky pet, we don't have all day. Three cans. That's my final offer!"

Rex thought for a moment and held out his paw to shake on the deal just as Alexa ran back into the bathroom with her Inspector Girl backpack fully loaded with supplies and then some, ready for action.

Pulling her hair into a pony tail with a pink satin scrunchy, she announced, "I'm ready!"

"It's about time," declared Jake, picking up the three cans of cat food, dumping them into her backpack. "Did you remember to pack the five gift certificates that Rupert gave us from The Library of Time to stop time in case we run into trouble?"

"Got them!" she exclaimed, putting the final touches to her hair.

Jake shouted with a happy grin, "**Then, let's go!**"

"But Jake," questioned Alexa "what about the barbeque? Won't everyone wonder where we are?"

"Don't worry, Lex," explained Jake. "Remember, Delbert said every time we go through the magnifying glass we will always return at the exact same moment we left. It'll be as if we never left."

"Are you sure?" she worried.

"Of course," he answered. "After all, Delbert is The Keeper of Time."

Jake grabbed the magnifying glass with the gusto of a world-class detective and thought about the case he needed to solve. As before, a small flicker of light glimmered on the cherry wood handle of the magnifying glass as the words appeared one by one.

Through the magnifying glass you will see,
the many misadventures that can be.

Jake grinned, remembering only a true detective could activate the magnifying glass, and that, of course, was he! The children then repeated the words three times out loud. The magnifying glass started to tremble in Jake's hand, falling to the bathroom floor. Upon hitting the granite floor, an enormous bolt of light sprang from the glass as it grew larger and larger. Suddenly, a huge wind tunnel shot out, blowing toilet paper and tissues all around the bathroom ceiling like ghosts on a Halloween hunt. The children smiled widely and laughed themselves silly as Rex jumped into the magnifying glass with yards of toilet paper clinging endlessly from his tail.

With her backpack firmly in place, Alexa grabbed Jake's hand, took a deep breath, and jumped with her big brother into the vortex of wind. They slid once again down the gigantic, seemingly endless slide, twisting and turning inside the magnifying glass, going faster and faster with every bend as sparkles of colorful stars flew past their wide open eyes.

Their fast and furious journey came to an end when they fell out of the magnifying glass, tumbling over each other and into a gigantic mound of hay piled high in the middle of an enormous, bright-red, wooden barn.

The magnifying glass let out another burst of light and shrunk back to its original size, clunking Jake on the head as it fell into the pile of hay. Rubbing his head and spitting out hay, Jake glared down at the magnifying glass. He saw an endless array of empty cardboard toilet paper tubes flying around the bathroom back home. The image rapidly began to fade into the magnifying glass and then, finally, disappeared from his sight.

CHAPTER THREE

A Surprise Guest

Startled, Jake stood up, frantically searching for Alexa. "Lexy! Lexy! Where are you?"

"I'm in here," she cried out in a muffled voice.

"Where—is here?" he bellowed.

"At the bottom of the pile of hay," she replied.

Jake frantically dove head first into the pile, digging and digging until he felt his sister. "Give me your hand," he yelled out. With a good, hard pull, he yanked her right out of the bristly tomb.

Alexa popped right out. "Thanks," she said as she removed the pieces of prickly hay poking into her body. "I just can't believe I did my hair right before we left. What a mess!" Alexa was rearranging her hair into a French twist when she noticed Rex was missing. "Where's Rex?" she screamed.

"Oh, no!" exclaimed Jake. "He must be buried alive in the hay."

"And you call yourself the world's greatest detective!" called Rex. *"I'm up here!"*

Jake and Alexa cleared the hay dust from their eyes and looked around the barn, which was covered wall-to-wall in hay and toilet paper. Remembering Rex could speak on this side of the magnifying glass, they followed the sound of his voice up to the vaulted, wood ceiling of the barn. To their shock and amusement, they found Rex dangling from toilet paper that was caught on an old horse saddle hanging from the rafters high above their heads.

"Rex, this is not the time to go bungee cord jumping. We have a case to solve," scolded Jake.

"Wow, that two-ply toilet paper really is strong!" announced Alexa.

"And ultra-absorbent, too!" replied Jake as he and Alexa fell back on the mound of hay, laughing themselves silly over Rex's predicament.

While swinging back and forth, Rex smirked, "*Very funny. When you two are done making a toilet paper commercial, you just might want to get me down from here!*"

"And just how did you get that toilet paper stuck on your tail, after all?" asked Jake.

Rex started to cut the paper ever-so-cautiously with his back paw. "*I've been experimenting with a new, super-absorbent, multi-cat, clumping, spring-scented litter. Apparently my experiment needs a little more work!*" With that said, the toilet paper snapped. "*Look out below!*" he warned, falling on top of them into the pile of hay.

Alexa stood up with Rex perched on top of her head and covered in hay. "Do you like my hat?" she asked.

Rex started moaning in pain as he jumped over to Jake's head, "*Ouch—ouch—sharp hay needles, piercing my delicate skin.*"

"Get off my head, you annoying fur ball!" yelled Jake, shaking his red hair wildly.

They all started pulling the hay off of each other in the middle of the barn. One by one, the golden yellow needles of hay fell to the dusty, knotty pine floor. As Alexa pulled the last needle from her hair, she cried, "Oh, no, my backpack is missing!"

"*Not again,*" groaned Rex. "*You lose that thing every time we fall out of the magnifying glass.*"

They all started to comb the barn for the backpack. Alexa started looking in the horse stalls while Rex looked behind an old, rickety wheelbarrow.

"*Boy, does it stink-a-rooney in here!*" observed Rex.

"It's a barn, you crazy cat. Animals do live here, you know," Jake scolded.

"*Well,*" snapped Rex. "*Apparently, they're not domesticated animals of the highest breeding and quality—like me!*"

Jake grabbed his magnifying glass from his back pocket and carefully searched the barn floor for any clues to the whereabouts of the missing backpack. "On a good day, your litter box smells worse than this!"

"*True, but I resemble that remark,*" declared Rex.

"It's 'resent,' not 'resemble'—you knucklehead!" corrected Jake.

"Do you guys see any sign of my backpack?" called out Alexa from the horse stalls.

"It's probably in the hay pile, Lexy. Don't worry, I'll get it," Jake said as he darted over to the pile of hay. As he got closer and closer, he examined each piece of hay with his magnifying glass. Suddenly, he noticed that something moved in the pile. "Rex, you're going to get all covered in hay again. Get out of there," he scolded.

"*What are you talking about?*" Rex questioned. "*I'm over here—behind the wheelbarrow.*"

Jake started to look a little worried. His long eyelashes brushed the cherry wood frame of the magnifying glass in anticipation of who or what was lurking in the pile of hay. "Lexy," he bellowed. "Where are you?"

"You don't have to shout," she answered. "I'm right behind you."

"Well, if Rex is over there—and you're behind me— who's in the hay?" Jake asked as he grabbed a rake hanging on the wall, ready to poke whatever was in the pile of hay.

"Jake!" Alexa cried out. "Be careful with that rake."

"I know how to handle a rake," he snapped.

From behind the wheelbarrow, Rex's golden eyes popped opened and his furry head puffed up like an overfilled furry balloon. "*Snake!*" he screamed. "*There's a snake.*"

"**SNAKE! WHAT SNAKE?**" Alexa screamed as she jumped behind the wheelbarrow, trembling in fear. "It's a snake!"

"W—w—h—ere—where's there a snake?" Jake stuttered as he dove behind the wheelbarrow, joining Rex and Alexa in a gigantic, trembling, bear hug of fear.

They all held on to each other, too afraid to move. "So where's the snake, Rex?" Jake asked.

"*I didn't see the snake,*" he answered. "*Alexa said 'snake.'*"

Alexa got a furious look on her face as her nose butted right up against his. They were staring right into each other's eyes. "I said, 'Jake, be careful with the rake,' and then I screamed 'snake' after you said 'snake.' "

"*Well, I heard someone say 'snake,'*" Rex said firmly as he hung his head low ashamed of his mistake.

"No, I said 'rake,' not 'snake,' you foolish puffball," roared Jake.

21

"*I thought you were going to take the rake to poke the snake. Then who saw the snake?*" Rex asked, now beet red from embarrassment.

"Apparently, no one, you foolish feline," quipped Jake. "I wasn't going to take the rake to poke the snake. I was using the rake to poke the object moving in the hay."

"*Then how do you now it's not a snake?*" questioned Rex.

"My keen detective skills are telling me it's—not, you nut ball!" declared Jake, putting his hands over his face in exasperation.

"Then why are we hiding behind this wheelbarrow?" Alexa responded.

"We're not," Jake answered as they all got up and crept over to the hay pile.

Rex saw the pink strap from Alexa's Inspector Girl backpack sticking out from the hay. Wanting to make amends for his snake foolishness, he jumped fearlessly into the pile and grabbed onto the strap in a tug of war with the culprit on the other end. "**Give it up, you dastardly fiend!**" he shrieked. "**GIVE IT UP!**" Rex pulled one way while the unknown thief pulled back the other. "*This guy's a strong little sucker!*" he yelled. Rex took one long, deep breath and pulled with all his might to release the backpack from the culprit's clutches. As the backpack snapped free, Rex went flying with it and the culprit across the barn, knocking into a pile of metal milking buckets.

Startled by the clatter, Jake and Alexa quickly ran over to the chaotic mess.

Rex was screaming for help with a milking bucket firmly stuck on his furry, rusty colored head.

"*Help! Help!*" he cried, licking droplets of milk from inside the bucket. "*Get this tin can off my head!*"

Jake and Alexa tugged and tugged on the bucket, trying to get it off.

"*Hey, watch out for my whiskers!*" he snapped.

"If you put your tongue back in your mouth, we'll have an easier time getting it off, you furry menace," Jake ordered. He then held onto the rim of the bucket and gave it a good twist and pull. Pop went the bucket, freeing Rex's slightly milk-matted head.

A little dazed from his ordeal, Rex started licking and grooming himself. His tongue didn't miss any of the drops dripping from his twisted whiskers, "***MMMMM—strawberry!***"

"See, Jake, strawberry milk in a barn!" announced Alexa.

"Just because there's strawberry milk in a milking bucket in a barn does not necessarily mean we're looking for pink cows!"

"*Looks that way to me!*" Rex agreed. "*But after all, I'm not The Great Inspector Moustachio.*"

Tossing her hair back in frustration, Alexa angrily yelled, "Well, apparently neither am I! Come Rex—I have a **PINK** brush in my **PINK** backpack that will brush out those knots full of **STRAWBERRY** milk from the non-existing **PINK COWS** we're supposedly not looking for." She grabbed her Inspector Girl backpack from the dusty barn floor and started digging through it in a huff, looking for the brush. "Now, where did I put that?" she asked herself.

"In the left zzz—z—zipper compartment," chutted a muffled voice from under one of the milking buckets. "*Who said that?"* questioned Rex as he crept over to the bucket, sniffing with feline curiosity.

There was a tiny knock from inside the bucket. "Isn't anyone going to let me out?" asked the faint voice.

They anxiously gathered around the bucket. Jake bent over and picked the milking bucket up in one swift swoop to reveal the unknown voice.

"**Sandy!**" they all screamed.

Alexa's short-haired, light-brown guinea pig, Sandy, came scooting out. "Hi ggg—g—guys!" she said in a sweet squeaky little voice.

Rex let out an unruly hiss and scoffed, "**Who invited her?**"

Alexa scooped her up and gave her the biggest kiss and hug. "Sandy, sweetie," she said, "whatever are you doing here?"

Sandy climbed up Alexa's arm and came to rest on her shoulder while nervously chattering her teeth. She took a short, little gasp of breath before explaining her tale to the puzzled group. "You guys had sss—s—so much fun when you went on your last misadventure to—now wait a second—it'll come to me—" Sandy thought and thought, but she just couldn't remember where they had gone. "What was the name of that place?" she asked.

"The Museum of Time—sweetie," explained Alexa. "Remember, I told that to you again this morning?"

"Oh, yeah—that's right. You saved time from—from—an—evil flower lady named Miss Tulip. Is that right?" Sandy guessed.

"No, my little munchkin," explained Alexa. "It was an evil food-poisoning, slicing and dicing cook by the name of

Mrs. Smythe who stole The Bell of Time."

"Oh, yeah—that's right," Sandy chutted. "Sorry! I just don't know why I can't rrr—r—remember things sometimes."

"It's O.K., Sandy" consoled Alexa. "Guinea pigs aren't supposed to have very good short-term memory. We'll fill you in as we go along!"

"Well, anyway," Sandy explained, "I felt left out, and I www—w—wanted to come and help this time, so I snuck into the backpack and stowed away for the ride. I promise I won't get in the way. Can I stay?" she said with a cheerful chut-chut-chut.

"Can she, Jake?" Alexa begged. "Please? Please?"

Rex stood up on his hind legs and shook his paw objecting, "*Certainly not! There's only one animal sidekick in this misadventure, and that oversized rodent is not going to steal my limelight— or my thunder!*"

"Wheep, Wheep," whistled Sandy in protest. "I'm not a rodent, you common alley cat. I am a princess guinea pig from Peru!"

Rex's eyes flashed in anger as he yelled, "*Well, then I guess I'm going to have a Peruvian delicacy for lunch when I slap you between two pieces of bread and smother you with mustard!*"

Jake paced back and forth, kicking the milking buckets, pondering the dilemma he was faced with. "Listen, you guys," he calmly explained, "we don't have time for this. We have to find Big Daddy and his cows to solve this mystery. Rex, there is only one Critter Detective and that's you. Sandy, if you promise to stay in the backpack and not get in the way, you can stay. Do we have a deal?"

Rex hissed while nodding his head yes.

Sandy whispered in Alexa's ear as she cheerfully chut-chut-chutted her way to the backpack. "I can't believe I can talk to you and you ccc—c—can understand me!"

"I know!" she explained. "Isn't it awesome? Some animals can talk on this side of the magnifying glass." Alexa then placed Sandy right into the front zippered compartment of the backpack, leaving the zipper wide open so they could chat up a storm.

"I just love the pink bedding your Mother bought for my cage. It's divine, and the adorable house www—w—with the yellow shutters is to die for," uttered Sandy.

"I know! I know!" answered Alexa as she placed a small pink bow on Sandy's head. "Isn't it beautiful?"

"Can you chat later? Hello—remember the missing cows we have to find?" Jake scolded.

"Sorry," the two little ladies said as they giggled and rubbed each other's noses.

"*You two are making me sick!*" complained Rex as he sniffed around the barn floor shaking his head in utter contempt.

As Jake kicked over the last bucket, he noticed something shimmering on the ground. "What's this?" he asked, picking it up to examine the sparkling object with his magnifying glass.

"It looks like a princess crown or a tiara of some kind!" Alexa explained, placing it on her head, prancing around like a beauty queen.

"*How could a fancy thing like that wind up in a stinky old barn like this?*" mumbled Rex.

"Rex," scolded Jake with an annoyed look, "what do you

have in your mouth? It better not be Sandy!"

"*Nothing!*" Rex mumbled as he took one gigantic swallow, followed by a huge burp.

"Now, you know the veterinarian said you're not supposed to eat weird things off the floor," declared Alexa. "You're going to get a tummy ache!"

"*No, I'm not!*" uttered Rex as his puffy furry cheeks turned shamefully red.

"Hey," said Jake, "after you almost got poisoned from Mrs. Smythe's lemon tarts at The Museum of Time, we can't be too careful."

"*Well, it was just a few lousy kernels of popcorn!*" Rex recalled. "*What do you expect? I'm a cat. That's what we do. We eat weird things off the floor.*"

"It's your stomach!" Jake snickered. "Eat what you want off the floor, but don't come crying to me if you get sick. Besides, you know what Dad always says about eating too much popcorn. '**It tastes good going down, but if you eat too much, too fast, it always gives you a stomach ache!**'"

Jake started to examine every speck of the crown, carefully looking for a clue to the owner and, possibly, the culprit guilty of the crime. In the center was a very distinct, black, metallic pearl surrounded by shimmering diamonds. "Well!" he muttered. "The thief who kidnapped the cows and caused milk to vanish from our breakfast tables and lunch boxes just might be a woman." Jake then handed the tiara back to Alexa so she could put it in her backpack for safekeeping. "And mum's the word to anyone we meet about this clue," ordered Jake. "We don't want to tip anyone off that we found it just yet."

"We're on the case, Inspector!" shouted Alexa as she handed the crown to Sandy, who crawled to the bottom of her Inspector Girl backpack and carefully slipped it into one of the hidden compartments.

Sandy then poked her head out of the backpack and chutted, "SSS—S—Safe and sound."

CHAPTER FOUR

The Auction

Suddenly, a blustery wind blew open the gigantic, red barn doors. A brilliant beam of sunlight blinded everyone until a large dark shadow covered their heads. They all trembled in fear as they heard the loud sound of big cowboy boots with big, clanking spurs getting closer and closer.

"I don't like the sound of that!" warned Jake, covering Alexa's eyes.

Trembling, Alexa did the same to Sandy's little brown eyes, crying out, "Maybe we should hide."

"*We're doomed! We're doomed!*" muttered Rex. "*We're as doomed as doomed can be!*"

In the doorway appeared the biggest cowboy the children had ever seen. He had a big, black moustache that spread for what seemed like yards across his face. His big, black hat reached up to the stars, and he walked in the biggest of black cowboy boots trimmed with shiny gold spurs tipped in silver. His red and white checkered shirt was neatly held into his big black pants by a big belt with an even bigger, solid gold belt buckle that read "***BIG DADDY***."

"*Wow!*" observed Rex. "*Now that is one BIG DUDE! BIGGER than BIG! BIG—BIG!*"

"What in tarnation happened to my barn?" yelled Big Daddy. "My big, beautiful, rootin' tootin' barn is smothered in toilet paper like flies on a horse's behind!"

"Now, that's not a pretty picture!" hissed Rex as everyone let out a sigh of relief, realizing the oversized cowboy was the voice that called upon them from the magnifying glass.

"Sorry, we had a really rough landing," explained Jake as he examined the lettering on Big Daddy's belt buckle with his magnifying glass.

"What did you expect?" Rex smirked. *"After all, you did call us when we were in the bathroom."*

"Well, I'm awful sorry, Inspector, that I wasn't here to greet y'all," explained Big Daddy. "I had a flood back at the house that I had to mop up. Bernardo, my prize bull, has been crying and crying and crying like a baby ever since the cows have been gone. He's been smitten for a while with a few of them, but I think he's especially fallen hard for a special one. Why, his big old heart is just broken to pieces! He's like a busted knob on a faucet. I just can't shut him off. His big, belly tears are flooding my house. Big Mama's trying to kick him off of the couch in the parlor and send him back to the barn, but he won't budge. He's just sitting there weeping away, making a spectacle of himself. I'm going to go crazy if I don't find those cows." Big Daddy stomped all around the barn looking in each and every stall like a hungry, ferocious lion searching for his prey. "So," he barked, "where are the cows?"

Jake paced back and forth, scratching his head while trying to come up with a suitable answer. Having figured out nothing on the case accept for finding the tiara, he stuttered, "W—w—ell, we're right on the case—it's—going great. I have lots of suspects."

Big Daddy was so excited to hear Jake's news that he

stomped his feet and tossed his twenty gallon cowboy hat right on top of Jake's head. "Well, my boy," he demanded, "tell me who that dastardly rascal is, and we'll hunt him down **together!**"

The size of Big Daddy's hat smothered Jake's face. Blinded by the darkness, he walked right into the open barn doors, knocking himself down onto the dusty wood floor. "Well, before we go hunting that dastardly rascal," he said as he pulled off the big, black hat and rolled it back to Big Daddy, "why don't we get all our ducks in a row and go over what happened right before the cows disappeared."

"That's a great idea," agreed Alexa and Rex while pulling Jake up from the ground.

"Details! Details! Details!" Alexa continued as Sandy handed her a shimmering, pink lip gloss from the backpack. She very carefully applied it to her very chapped lips and said, "The Great Inspector Moustachio always needs details before solving the crime."

"You mean more time! More time! More time!" hissed Rex into Jake's ear. *"We have nothing!"*

"Remember, my furry little friend," whispered back Jake, "Grandpa used to say ' **the greatest gift in life is the power to believe,**' and I believe I will solve this mystery with a little more time."

"Time we have plenty of!" Rex scoffed back. *"It's clues and suspects we're fresh out of."*

Big Daddy started to pull down all the scattered toilet paper from the rafters of the barn. As he began to roll it into a ball, he started to tell the story of his doggone missing cows.

"Well, three days ago we were all at the county fair. I

always like to make hay while the sun shines, so I got there real early to examine the cows before the livestock auction. I always buy some new cows this time of year. The auction was just about to begin. The auctioneer was bringing in the next lot of cows to be inspected when a strange looking Indian chief appeared out of nowhere calling himself Buffalo Hump. He offered to sell me some prime, ace-high cows at a bargain. Everyone knows how I just love a great deal. That's how I got the name Big Daddy. As I forked over the money, he whispered something strange into my ear, ' **When the pale moon rises in front of the sun god, the path to a sacred Indian ground will be revealed on the hide of the chosen cow. Treasures will await you at the end of your journey.**' "

"My mind might be a little foggy sometimes, but exactly what does that gibberish mmm—m—mean?" asked Sandy.

"*Is it my crazy cat brain's imagination, or does this story sound vaguely familiar?*" Rex questioned as he grabbed some toilet paper and added it to Big Daddy's growing ball.

Jake and Alexa paid no attention to Rex. Jake grabbed the rake and started gathering up the loose toilet paper as Alexa added it into the ever-growing ball. "Well," Jake thought out loud, "obviously one of the cows has some sort of secret code or patterned map on its hide that will allow us to figure out where the treasure is."

"But why would the Indian Chief give up his cows and a treasure?" asked Alexa, cleaning up behind the stalls. "It just doesn't make any sense."

"Maybe the Indian can't go to the sacred ground on his own," Jake surmised.

Sandy popped out of the Inspector Girl backpack and scurried all around the barn, helping to pick up some toilet paper. "He might need someone else to do it for him!" she suggested.

"The rodent has a good point!" Rex stubbornly agreed. *"But what does a 'pale moon rising in front of a sun god' mean?"*

"I'm not sure," answered Jake. "We definitely have some missing pieces to this mysterious puzzle."

"Well, if anyone can figure it out," Alexa declared, "it's The Great Inspector Moustachio!"

Sandy gathered up a bunch of toilet paper and jumped on top of the growing ball. She noticed a small ticket stub mixed in with the paper she was stuffing into the gigantic ball. "Jake—Jake!" she yelled from above.

"Not now, Sandy," he snapped. "We're trying to make sense of this puzzle."

"BBB—B—But Jake!" she chutted.

Alexa gave Sandy a disapproving eye, warning her not to disturb Jake during his investigation.

Sandy ever-so-quietly continued to push every loose piece of toilet paper into the ball, including the ticket stub, which eventually disappeared under the many layers of toilet paper.

"Which cow do you think had the information to the treasure on its hide, Big Daddy?" asked Jake.

"I haven't got the foggiest idea. They all look alike to me. Ya' got your white cows, your brown cows, and your pink cows," answered Big Daddy. "I thought the Indian Chief would be cooling his heels for a while after the auction so I could ask him that exact same question, but he vanished into thin air."

"Ahhh haaa!" announced Alexa anxiously. "I knew it! Tell us, Big Daddy, what flavor of milk comes out of each of those cows?"

"Well, little lady, don't get your dander up," he hollered. "Why everyone knows cow juice comes in three flavors: chocolate cow juice from brown cows, white cow juice from white cows, and strawberry cow juice from the pinkest of the pink ones."

Alexa just stood there next to the eight-foot ball of toilet paper with an enormous smile of satisfaction on her face at having proven her brother wrong. "I'll believe it when I see it," Jake grunted, still in disbelief.

"Well, Inspector, it looks like you're fit to be tied," consoled Big Daddy. "But it's true! Ya' know things are always a little strange on this side of the magnifying glass."

"Did anyone hear or see Buffalo Hump talking to you?" asked Jake as he started to roll the ball towards the barn doors.

"There was my nephew and ranch hand, Bob Billy Bob. He was tipping over the sleeping cows for fun just before the auction started. I doubt he noticed anything. Ya' know—he's slower than a sleeping turtle, but he's always been a loyal and helpful cowhand. There's just no way he's the scallywag who stole my cows."

"He may not be as sweet and as loyal as you think!" declared Alexa.

"You might have a point there, pretty lady," said Big Daddy. "The boy doesn't have a plumb nickel to rub together, and he's been hounding me for a raise lately. I think he might be fixin' to take a bride. He keeps disappearing on me when there's work to be done!"

"The thought of finding a lost treasure can make the nicest of people do the nastiest of things," suggested Rex.

"When did you notice the cows missing?" asked Alexa.

"That evening after we tucked our baby boy, Little Big Daddy, in for the night. Big Mama and I came out here to the barn to give all the cows their supper. The barn doors were wide open, and my cows were gone!"

"Could anyone else at the auction have overheard you and Buffalo Hump talking?" asked Jake as he and Alexa rolled the ball into the doorway.

"Well, I do remember seeing Miss Sally-Mae McGraw and her Goat Baron Daddy, Rufus McGraw. That man is crazier than a pig in a mud bath. He owns the largest goat ranch in these parts, right over there," Big Daddy explained, pointing out the barn window to the Giddy Goat Ranch's fields that lay beyond the rambling river.

"Well, goats do make milk, right?" chutted Sandy.

"The goats at the Giddy Goat Ranch make him the biggest toad in the puddle when it comes to goat juice," proclaimed Big Daddy.

"By getting rid of all the cows, he would be getting rid of all the cow milk," explained Jake.

"Then he would be able to sell everyone his goat milk and become bigger than you," said Rex to Big Daddy.

Big Daddy stomped over to the enormous ball of toilet paper and plucked Rex right off the top. He grabbed him by the end of his tail, dangling him like a yo-yo, looked him square in the eyes, and snarled, "There's nobody ***BIGGER*** than Big Daddy, little fella'!"

Trembling in fear, the fur on Rex's tail puffed up as Big

Daddy then let him down with a gentle thud.

"What about Miss Sally-Mae?" Alexa asked.

"Miss Sally-Mae had just won a first prize blue ribbon for the prettiest pig at the fair's Miss Piggly Wiggly Beauty Pageant," he said.

Rex was rolling around on the floor, laughing himself silly. *"Well, I can't wait to get a good look at her!"* he joked.

The gigantic ball of toilet paper was now stuck in the doorway. Jake and Alexa tried to squeeze it through as Sandy and Rex jumped up and down on top, trying to make it smaller.

"She had a bee in her bonnet dancing all around the auction, waving that darn blue ribbon in her father's face when he was trying to inspect the animals," said Big Daddy, kicking the ball right out of the barn with his big, black boot with the silver tip. "Sally-Mae was whining how she wanted to open up a pig grooming parlor to make all the pigs in the world the prettiest they could be. Rufus is a penny dreadful man. Why—he's so cheap he still has the first penny he ever made. He told her there was no way he was giving her any money for such foolishness. She made a spectacle of herself, grabbing her pig, Magnolia, and stomping out of the auction in a big old huff."

"Well, then," said Jake, "she needed money. If she heard about the treasure, she just might have been mad enough to kidnap your cows. We need to go check out the Giddy Goat Ranch and look for clues."

Just as they were about to leave the barn, Big Daddy stopped dead in his tracks remembering something else from the auction.

"Inspector," he said, "I do recall an odd looking fella', a stranger to these parts, I reckon. He was sneaking around the auction acting very nervous, worse than a long tailed cat in a room full of rocking chairs. He had on a long, yellow, linen duster. Why, that coat draped all over him like a magician's cape. He had an odd flat-brimmed hat that sat tilted on his head. It slightly covered a jagged scar running through his tiny, black moustache on the right side of his face. Why, that scar's shape almost reminded me of the letter *M.* His black pants were tucked real tight into his high, shiny black boots, and there was something sticking out of the left one."

"What was it?" asked Alexa as she grabbed her backpack.

Big Daddy took his hat off, scratching his head to recall. "It looked like a small book of some sort."

"That's a strange place to put a book," added Rex.

"And even more curious for an unknown outsider to be at that auction," suggested Jake.

"Do you think he kidnapped the cows, Jake?" asked Alexa.

"I'm not sure," he said. "But my keen detective skills are telling me that he's definitely trouble. What was it you wanted to tell me, Sandy?" Jake asked.

Sandy just stood there thinking and thinking and thinking. She couldn't remember the ticket stub that she found earlier or its final destination inside the gigantic ball of toilet paper. "I—I— just can't remember!" she said with a sad look in her tiny, brown eyes.

"It's O.K., sweetie," consoled Alexa as she picked Sandy up and gave her a little hug and a kiss on her tiny head.

"Well, it couldn't have been that important anyway,"

snarled Rex. *"After all—she's just a pig!"*

Sandy glared at Rex with disapproving eyes.

"I know—I know," he smirked. *"You're a guinea pig from Peru, not a pig—pig, but a guinea pig! Yeah—Yeah—Yeah."*

CHAPTER FIVE

Bull's Eye

Just outside Big Daddy's barn was the cows' grazing field all covered with the greenest grass the children had ever seen. It was surrounded by a white picket fence with an open gate that the gigantic ball of toilet paper had rolled into. Sitting on top of the ball was Bernardo, crying his eyes out over the lost cows. Bernardo was a big bull with a long, bristly, brown coat and a big, brass ring dangling from his nose. A handsome blue and white, striped bandana was firmly knotted around his thick neck. Long, pointy horns that spanned from ear to ear framed his face.

"Bernardo!" Big Daddy yelled. "Stop crying. You're flooding my fields with all that bellyaching."

Bernardo was a mess! He was blowing his snout on the loose toilet paper hanging off the ball. But he couldn't stop crying and crying.

"There, there, Bernardo," consoled Alexa as she stroked his chin. "My brother is the world's greatest detective. He'll find the cows." Bernardo just let out a hysterical cry and blew his nose loudly into the ball.

"*That is one sad bully,*" declared Rex, jumping up on the fence.

"He's a bull—not a bully, you confused cat," corrected Jake.

While Big Daddy was trying to get Bernardo to

stop crying, Jake was carefully exploring the outside of the barn for any clues that might lead him to the culprit who kidnapped the cows. He walked all around the fence, examining every inch with the magnifying glass. As Rex followed along on top of the fence, he came to a broken piece of fencing and jumped off into the field of tall grass.

"*Ouch!*" he cried, limping along in pain.

Jake and Alexa came rushing to his aid, yelling, "What happened?"

"*I jumped on something sharp and cut my paw,*" he cried. "*I have a boo-boo!*"

Alexa immediately opened up her Inspector Girl backpack, which was always filled with endless, unusual treasures. Sandy dug deep to the bottom and popped up with a band-aid for Rex's paw. "Ahh, yes!" exclaimed Alexa. "Never leave home without your first aid kit."

"*You wouldn't happen to have a doctor in there?*" moaned Rex. "*Would ya'?*"

"I'll check," smirked Jake as he rolled his eyes at the tiny scratch on Rex's paw.

Alexa began to bandage Rex's cut. "Hold still, Rexy Cat," she said firmly.

"*I can't look!*" he groaned. "*The sight of blood makes me woozy.*"

"It's a scratch, you scaredy cat," scolded Jake. "Stop making a mountain out of a mole hill!"

Jake used his magnifying glass to examine the area of grass where Rex cut himself while Alexa finished bandaging Rex's paw.

Jake bent over and picked up a sharp metal object buried deep within the blades of grass. "What's this?" he questioned.

"It's a bell!" declared Alexa.

Jake zoomed in with the magnifying glass and saw a painted pink flower on a square–shaped, silver bell.

"*Now, where do you suppose that came from?*" Rex asked, limping around on three paws.

"More importantly," surmised Jake, "who does it belong to?" Jake shoved the bell into his pocket and jumped over the white fence, running as fast as he could to Big Daddy, who was still trying to get Bernardo to move off of the big ball of toilet paper and stop his endless crying over the lost cows. Just then, a shadow passed over Jake's head. Looking up, he noticed a light-brown hawk soaring high in the sun-drenched sky. Alexa followed fast behind with Sandy bouncing up and down in her Inspector Girl backpack.

"*Wait for me!*" cried Rex as he leaped along. "*You know, this band-aid feels pretty good. It's a miracle— I'm cured!*"

"Big Daddy," Jake asked, "do any of your animals wear bells?"

Big Daddy thought for awhile and after a long pause answered, "Well, I used to have a rooster by the name of Dusty. He always wore a bell around his scrawny, red-feathered neck. He'd ring it like the dickens, right before he'd yell **COCK-A-DOODLE –DOO** every morning!"

"What happened to Dusty?" Alexa asked.

"Well, pretty lady," explained Big Daddy, "it broke my heart, but I just had to give him away. Once me and the Missus had Little Big Daddy, there was going to be no more noise at four o'clock in the morning waking us all up. A new baby's gotta' get his sleep, ya' know."

"Oh, that is soooooo true!" exclaimed Alexa as she

grabbed two pink ribbons from Sandy and tied two pigtails in her hair. "My friend, Grace, just has to have her full eight hours of beauty sleep every night or else she is one cranky girl!"

Jake pulled the bell out from his pants pocket and showed it to Big Daddy. "Is this Dusty's bell?" he asked.

Big Daddy laughed himself silly. "My boy, that's not a rooster bell—it's a goat bell!"

Jake, Alexa, and Rex all looked at each other with satisfied grins, having just found another clue to help solve the case.

"That bell must belong to the Giddy Goat Ranch!" exclaimed Alexa.

"You're right!" said Jake as he handed the clue to Alexa. "The culprit who took the cows must have dropped it when they ran from the scene of the crime."

Alexa handed the bell to Sandy, who placed it at the bottom of the backpack right next to the tiara the children had found earlier.

"We need to get to the Giddy Goat Ranch to search for more clues that might lead us to the cows," said Jake.

"*I can't possibly walk that far with my bruised paw,*" moaned Rex, lying helplessly in the high green blades of grass.

"It's a long way by foot," bellowed Big Daddy as he wiped the tears from Bernardo's eyes with a loose piece of toilet paper from the ball. "But it'll be two whoops and a holler if Bernardo takes ya' there! I reckon you could be there in less than fifteen minutes with Bernardo at top speed."

"*I think we'd better find a way to drag him off that darn ball first,*" reminded Rex.

Alexa searched through her backpack and pulled out a Clunky Chunky Chocolate Bar. "How about it, Bernardo?" asked Alexa as she waved the caramel crusted milk chocolate bar under his nose.

"*Hey,*" yelled Rex as he sprang up on all fours, "*you were saving that for me!*"

"Desperate times call for desperate measures," declared Alexa.

"And these are the most desperate of times, little fella'," proclaimed Big Daddy.

"Listen, you whiney, whisker head," scolded Jake. "Without the cows, there will be no more milk chocolate. And that will be the last Clunky Chunky Chocolate Bar you'll ever get to see. Let the bull have it if it gets him off that darn ball. We'll find the cows, replenish the milk supply, and then you can have all the Clunky Chunkys you want when we get home—*DEAL?*"

"*Oh—all right!*" sniped Rex as he limped off in a huff.

Alexa continued to wave the bar under Bernardo's nose. "Come on Bernardo," she coaxed. "It's **delicious!**"

Bernardo was rocking back and forth on the gigantic ball of toilet paper, pondering his options.

Big Daddy had had enough of Bernardo's crying. He took off his tall, twenty gallon hat and waved it high into the sky as he stomped frantically around the ball. He angrily glared at Bernardo, straight into his big, wet, puffy, bloodshot eyes. "Bernardo," warned Big Daddy, "if you don't get the heck down from that toilet paper ball, the next time we go to the rodeo, I'm gonna dress ya' up in a pink and purple bandana covered in bright yellow flowers."

Sandy popped her head out of the Inspector Girl

backpack and chutted, "WWW-W—Well, that sounds pretty to me!"

"*Not to a manly bull, it's not,*" laughed Rex.

Bernardo awkwardly slid off the ball and grumbled under his breath as he ate the Clunky Chunky Chocolate Bar, "**O.K.**"

CHAPTER SIX

Up The River

Big Daddy bent down and picked up Alexa ever-so-gently, placing her on top of Bernardo's back. Jake jumped right up as Rex scurried up Bernardo's tail.

"Well, I think you're all rarin' to go," shouted Big Daddy. "While y'all investigate the Giddy Goat Ranch, I'm going to run on back to the house. Bob Billy Bob and I are working on my barbeque sauce recipe. It's almost perfect. We just have to figure out what's missing. I'm going to be the biggest barbeque sauce king there ever was and will ever be. Why, I may become more famous for my barbeque sauce then I am for my grade-A cow milk. Bernardo, when the Inspector is done, bring 'em all back for some grub. I'm gonna rustle us up some spareribs smothered in my secret sauce. It'll be waiting for y'all!"

Alexa had the widest smile spread across her face. "Spareribs!" she screamed out in excitement. "I just love spareribs—they're my favorite food of all time! You know, my grandma's been trying to get my great-great-grandma Mary's barbeque sauce recipe just right for years, but she's been having trouble with the last couple of ingredients, too!"

Rex started licking his lips in anticipation of devouring the ribs as he slid back down Bernardo's tail to the ground.

"Just where do you think you're going?" Jake asked

from above with a wrinkle in his forehead.

"*I'm starving,*" sighed Rex. "*I'm going back to Big Daddy's for some grub.*"

"Think again, you annoying fur ball." Jake said angrily.

"*Let me guess,*" Rex annoyingly responded, "*I'm getting back up on this gigantic bull and going off to search for the cows—aren't I?*"

"You bet your tail, you are!" proclaimed Jake. "Besides, we packed three cans of cat food just before we left. You can have a snack later."

Rex climbed back up Bernardo's tail. "*Now, let me get this straight. You think I would rather eat canned cat food instead of barbequed spareribs?*" he asked.

"Well, it wasn't dog food you packed," Jake answered with a stern look.

"*You have a point!*" snapped Rex.

Jake told Bernardo they were ready to start their journey. As they set out, Big Daddy rolled the gigantic, eight-foot ball of toilet paper out of the grazing field and rested it up against a large weeping willow tree high up on the hill just around the corner from the back of the barn. He then headed up to the house to find Bob Billy Bob.

"Bob Billy Bob!" he called out in a huff. "Where the heck are ya' now? Why, I swear if his arms weren't hanging from his shoulders, he'd probably lose 'em!"

With Sandy stowed snuggly away in Alexa's backpack, they bopped up and down on Bernardo's bristly back. Bernardo headed up the river towards the Giddy Goat Ranch, still sniffling over the lost cows. His horns dragged low as his head drooped to the ground, knocking into every prickly, bright-green cactus plant that crossed his path.

"*Riding a snail would be faster than this,*" snapped Rex.

Stroking Bernardo's back, Alexa said softly, "He can't help it. He's lost the loves of his life."

"As sad as that is, Lexy," Jake added, "at this speed, we won't be getting to the Giddy Goat Ranch any time soon."

"*This is utterly ridiculous,*" fussed Rex as he bounced up and down on Bernardo's back. "*I think a turtle just ran past us!*"

"Oh—Rexy Cat," sighed Alexa as she wiped Bernardo's tears with a pink and purple scarf she found in the secret compartment of her backpack. "You have to be patient. We'll get there, eventually."

"*Easy for you to say,*" snapped Rex. "*I'm going to need a litter box real soon, and we're stuck in the middle of nowhere riding on top of a crying bull, looking for kidnapped cows who will supposedly lead us to a lost treasure, and all we have to go on is a goat bell and a princess's crown.*"

"It's not a princess's crown," chirped Sandy as she popped her head out of the backpack. "It's a tiara that beauty queens wear."

"*Are you still here!*" Rex demanded angrily. "*I thought that pig got buried in that gigantic ball of toilet paper and was gone for good.*"

"You should bbb—b—be so lucky," snapped Sandy. "You're always trying to get attention, and I'm not a pig! I'm a guinea pig, you hairy clod! From, where am I from again? I—forgot!"

"Peru, sweetie," Alexa reminded. "Peru."

"*Me?*" yelled Rex. "*What about you? You're always*

sitting on top of Grandma Mustachio's lap, looking for a snuggle and a kiss."

"You're just jealous," exclaimed Sandy, "because she likes me better than you!"

"Does not!"

"Does too!"

"Hey, you two in the backseat," scolded Jake as he held onto Bernardo's horns. "Knock it off. I'm trying to drive the bull, and your arguing is distracting me. We're going to get into an accident."

"Distract you from what?" snickered Rex. *"There's nothing around here for miles and miles but dust and cactus plants. That darn, blazing sun's making me hotter than a burger on a barbeque."*

Bernardo slowly crept his way up the river towards the Giddy Goat Ranch.

Alexa gave Bernardo a big snuggle and asked, "Couldn't you go a little faster, my big strong bull?"

"This is getting us nowhere!" shouted Rex as he grabbed firmly onto Bernardo's tail. *"I know just what to do!"*

Jake glared back to Rex and warned him, "Don't do it Rex! You're going to regret it."

Rex stood up on his hind legs and, with a mischievous grin on his face, yanked on Bernardo's tail screaming, *"The cows! The cows! They're at the Giddy Goat Ranch!"*

"Ahhh—ohhh!" cried Jake. "Hold on, Lexy!"

Bernardo raised his head, causing his pointy, ivory horns to shine brightly from the reflection of the sunlight high in the sky. His big, brown eyes popped open as wide as could be. "**COOOOOWS?**" he bellowed. Steam shot out of his nose as he raised his hooves and started to charge crazily up the river toward the ranch.

"Ahhhhhhhh!" screamed the children as they held on for their young lives. Bernardo jumped right into the shallow waters of the winding, rambling river, increasing his speed with every turn. Tiny river rocks flew around like bullets as he kicked them out of his way.

One of the river rocks clunked Rex right on top of his head. "*Ouch!*" he cried as he started to slide off the back end of Bernardo. "*Help! Help!*" Rex cried out in sheer terror.

The children were bouncing around as if they were sitting in a run-away roller coaster.

Jake held out his hand, trying to keep Rex from falling. "Give me your paw," he screamed as the forceful wind blew against their faces.

Rex tried to stretch out his paw, but he couldn't reach him. Alexa frantically pleaded with Bernardo to slow down, but he couldn't hear her due to the splashing of the water and shooting rocks from the riverbed. Besides, nothing was going to stop him from being reunited with his cows.

"*I'm doomed!*" cried Rex as he started to slip over the side.

Bernardo hit a huge rock and they all went flying into the air. "Wooooooow!" they shouted. Alexa's backpack strap got hooked on Bernardo's right horn, giving Sandy a front row seat to all the chaos. She let out a screeching, fearful chutter and hid at the bottom of the Inspector Girl backpack. Alexa and Jake started to fall but bounced back onto Bernardo's back. Rex made a frantic attempt to grab on to Bernardo's tail. He missed, but the bandage from his paw got stuck on the tip of Bernardo's bristly tail, leaving him dangling from the end.

"Ouch! Ouch! Ouch!" Rex cried as Bernardo dragged him up the river at full speed. *"Is this band-aid waterproof?"* he asked.

Looking back at him, Jake screamed through the wind, "You'd better hope so!"

Jake tried to grab hold of Bernardo's horns to slow him down, without any luck. He was gaining speed as he made his way up the river.

"Sandy," cried out Alexa, "are you all right, sweetie? Hold on!"

Sandy crawled up the tiara to the top of the bouncing backpack, unzipped herself and poked her head out just enough to answer. "I—I—think so," she said. "By the way—I forgot—why are we riding on a bull?"

"I'll remind you later!" shouted Alexa. "Get back down!" she warned, bouncing all over the place.

"Who cares about that stupid pig," screeched Rex. The band-aid was stretching and stretching with every bounce as he was dragged for miles over the river rocks. *"This band-aid isn't going to hold much longer."*

"You always said you wanted to learn how to water ski," yelled Jake through the wind. "Now's your chance!"

"Jake, look!" exclaimed Alexa, pointing towards the top of the hill. "It's the Giddy Goat Ranch."

Rex was soaking wet from being dragged through the river. He prayed Bernardo would slow down, but he just went faster and faster as he approached the gates to the ranch.

"Bernardo, slow down!" demanded Jake as he pulled back on his horns with all his strength.

"Stop—Bernardo! Stop!" cried Alexa. "We're going to crash into the gates."

"Oh—no!" yelled Jake. "**Duck!**"

Screaming, they all ducked down low. Bernardo stormed the tall wooden gates to the Giddy Goat Ranch. The force of his entry sent shredded wood flying high into the sky.

Jake looked up and saw that they were headed straight for a big, old, muddy pig pen. He noticed a pile of bright, green-colored hay directly to his right. "Jump, you guys! Jump!" he ordered.

Alexa quickly grabbed Sandy and her backpack with her left hand as Jake grabbed her right hand. They dove into the pile of hay. Rex was frantically trying to rip the band-aid from his paw, without any luck. Bernardo, realizing he was headed straight for the pig pen, came to an abrupt stop. His tail quickly snapped from behind him, stretching the band-aid with Rex soaring towards the sky.

"*Noooooo!*" cried out Rex. As the bandage ripped, he was catapulted like a stone from a slingshot towards the pig pen, with his arms and legs spread out like an eagle's wings. With his eyes open as wide as his mouth, in shock, he landed face down, right in the middle of the muddiest, old pig pen. He lifted his pathetic, little, fuzzy, mud-drenched face up for a second and whimpered in disgust, "*I hate pigs!*"

CHAPTER SEVEN

The Two Old Goats

Jake and Alexa crawled out of the pile of green hay. "Are you O.K., Jake?" she asked as she dug down deeply into the hay for her Inspector Girl backpack and her beloved Sandy.

"That was a close call," uttered Jake, brushing the green hay from his clothes.

"Yeah!" exclaimed Alexa. "I thought we were goners!"

Bernardo came crawling by, still looking as sad as sad could be over his lost cows. He walked up the hill towards the meadow, sat down on a large boulder in frustration, and cried like a baby.

"What are we going to do about him?" asked Alexa.

"We'll have to deal with him later," explained Jake. "We should take care of Rex first, and we do have a case to solve."

"You're right, Inspector," said Alexa. "The clues await us!"

Jake and Alexa ran over to the pig pen where Rex was still lying face down, drenched in mud.

"Why is it every time I tell you not to do something that I'm sure is going to end badly, you do it anyway, you crazy fur ball?" scolded Jake.

Rex lifted his head again from the mud and answered, *"I guess screaming out '**the cows were at the ranch**' wasn't such a good idea."*

"You think!" replied Jake with a raised eyebrow and a smirk across his face. "By the way, are you planning to get out of that pig pen any time soon?"

Rex, covered head to toe in drippy, wet mud, slinked out of the pig pen in complete humiliation.

The pig pen was just outside of a small, pink, wood barn. It had a white roof with tall windows framed in purple shutters. Under each of the open windows were hot-pink window boxes overflowing with the most beautiful, white and pink flowers the children had ever seen. Jake snatched his magnifying glass from his back pocket and started to examine each and every one of the flowers for more clues to solve the case.

"Is it my imagination," he questioned, "or are these flowers the same as the one on the goat bell?"

Alexa immediately unzipped her Inspector Girl backpack. "Sandy," she said, "hand me that bell we found, sweetie."

Sandy dove to the bottom and pulled up the bell and handed it to Alexa. She then jumped out of the backpack to explore the strange surroundings for herself.

"Don't wander too far off, Sandy," said Alexa as she carefully examined the bell before she handed it to Jake. "I'm not sure," she murmured with a curious grin. "The flowers do look alike."

Jake examined the bell's flower and compared it to the ones in the window boxes. "I'm sure this flower's shape is the same as these," he continued. He then placed the goat bell back into Alexa's backpack for safekeeping.

"Then that bell must have come from here," nodded Alexa.

As Rex tried to shake off the mud, he demanded, *"What kind of stinky flowers are those, anyway?"*

"MAGNOLIAS, YOU SILLY BOY!" shouted a voice from inside one of the windows of the barn. "Why, everyone knows that, of course!"

From out of the lower left window popped a beautiful woman wearing a pink, flowered sundress. She had pale, white skin and the most beautiful, crystal-clear, sparkling, blue eyes they had ever seen. A tiara, just like the one they found at Big Daddy's barn, was placed ever-so-neatly in her perfectly–combed, long, black, flowing hair.

"Aren't you just the cutest bunch of children my pretty, blue eyes have ever seen?" she said with a wild look in them. "Don't you move your cute little feet—I'll bring my pretty self right out to you!"

As the children waited for the peculiar woman to come out from the barn, Sandy went roaming about the ranch on her own. A few yards from the barn, she stumbled upon a house where two goat heads were mounted on either side of the front door.

"Oh, my!" said the one white goat.

"I know, dear!" nodded the gray one.

"Isn't it awful?" added the white one.

"I just can't believe it!" agreed the gray goat.

"What's the matter?" asked Sandy, looking up at the two goats with a little smile across her tiny face.

"Did you hear something, dear?" asked the white goat to the gray one.

"I'm not sure!" replied the gray one to the white one.

"I think my hearing is going!" said the white goat to the gray.

"Down here!" chutted Sandy.

The two goats looked down to the ground and said together with a smile, "Well, hello there."

"Yes, hello to you from me!" said the white goat.

"And a hello from me to you, too!" said the gray one.

"MMM—M—My name is Sandy. Who are you?" she asked.

"Why, I'm Fannie," answered the white goat.

"And I'm Annie," added the gray one.

With a huge smile and a ringing of both the bells around their necks they sang, "We're the Nanny Goat sisters, Fannie and Annie."

"Rufus McGraw mounted us up here to keep an eye on his goats, don't you know?" said Fannie.

"He doesn't want his goats to get kidnapped like Big Daddy's cows," said Annie.

"Oh, no, that would be dreadful!" agreed Fannie. "One moment, dears. I'm getting a message in my head. Oh, dear, that's even worse than we thought."

"What's the matter?" asked Sandy.

"Haven't you heard?" cackled Annie.

"Heard what?" questioned Sandy.

"Well," explained Fannie, "Jasper, the mounted moose head at The Museum of Time, told Rocco, the mounted rhinoceros head at the zoo in Antwerp, who told Penelope, the mounted ostrich head that hangs around the amusement pier at Pirate's Point, who told **US** that the crazy cake-poisoning cook, Mrs. Smythe, who was put in prison for stealing **Time,** has—**ESCAPED!**"

"Escaped!" exclaimed Sandy in terror.

"That's what my sister said, dear—escaped," uttered

nie. "Gerard, the mounted giraffe head, who's the
_ ard at the prison, was watching Mrs. Smythe while she
was baking lemon tarts for the other prisoners. When out
of nowhere, an enormous bolt of lightning exploded, and a
huge vortex of wind started to blow right inside the prison—
don't you know? Then, from out of thin air, an evil-looking
man with an *M*-shaped scar running through the tiny, black
moustache on his face appeared, don't you know? Before he
took Mrs. Smythe by the hand and escaped into the vortex of
wind, she tied Gerard's extra long neck into a gigantic knot
to prevent him from telling anyone what happened."

"ThThTh-Th—That's awful," chutted Sandy.

"It took them forever to untie him!" continued Fannie.

"Imagine that!" exclaimed Annie.

"Oh, boy!" jabbered Sandy, "I need to tell Jake and Alexa
all about this right away! I'm going to prove I can be just as
good a detective as that nasty cat, Rex!"

"And so you should, my dear," baahed the Nanny Goats
sisters, ringing their bells. "And so you should!"

Excitement was beaming from her teeny-tiny, brown
eyes as Sandy darted off across the pasture of the Giddy
Goat Ranch back to the muddy pig pen and her pals. "See ya'
later," she called out to the sisters. "I hope I can keep this in
my head long enough to tell someone!" she mumbled.

Sandy reached the pig pen just as Jake was walking all
around the pink barn looking for more clues. Through his
magnifying glass, he noticed a few bright-yellow pieces of
hay sprinkled across the ground.

"Jake! Jake!" shouted Sandy, bouncing all around. "I
have some nnn—n—news to tell you."

Jake was so busy inspecting the yellow hay he didn't

even notice Sandy jumping all around him.

"That's odd," he thought out loud. "The hay we jumped into by the pig pen over there was green. This hay is yellow, like the kind in Big Daddy's cow barn."

"Jake! Jake!" shouted Sandy.

"Not now, Sandy!" snapped Jake as he gathered up the yellow hay and ran back to Alexa. "I think I just found a very important clue."

Alexa was trying to clean off some of the mud from Rex's fur. "Hold still!" she scolded brushing his tangled fur.

"*Ouch!*" moaned Rex.

"Hey, you guys," shouted Jake as he showed them the hay. "Look what I found."

"*You found hay,*" sneered Rex. "*Wow, you really are the world's greatest detective.*" Rex bent down and picked up a pile of hay from the ground. "*I found hay, too! Now I'm the world's greatest detective!*"

Jake got a very annoyed look on his face as he glared angrily at Rex, "Listen, you mangy fur ball, your hay is green."

"*And your point is—?*" asked Rex.

"The hay I found is yellow," replied Jake.

"*So—,*" smirked Rex.

"Look around, you foolish feline," said Jake. "All the hay here at the Giddy Goat Ranch is green—alfalfa hay. It's the best food for goats and horses. All the hay at Big Daddy's cow barn was yellow, probably aged Timothy Hay. Cows love to eat that stuff. Yellow hay shouldn't be here unless someone brought it here. That means whoever kidnapped the cows might have hidden them somewhere here and, without knowing it, accidentally dropped the hay."

"The mystery unfolds!" whispered Alexa.

"*So, you're saying the yellow hay might have fallen off the culprit's body or off the stolen cows' hides,*" Rex deducted, caressing his whiskers.

"I can't prove it yet," proclaimed Jake with a suspicious grin. "But I'll bet the culprit and those cows are somewhere here."

"And that's why he's the world's greatest detective," announced Alexa as she put the yellow hay in her backpack.

Just as Sandy reached the children, the double-hung, white barn doors flew open and the unusual, black-haired woman burst through the doorway.

"Guys, Guys," chutted Sandy, "I have something ttt—t— to tell you!"

"Not now, sweetie," said Alexa as she rolled her favorite pink lip gloss across her dry lips. Tying a new, pink, satin ribbon in her hair, she added anxiously, "We're about to find out who the mysterious lady is with the tiara."

Rex, with an evil grin, bent down and butted his nose up against Sandy's head. She could smell the tuna surprise he had for breakfast on his breath. "*Why don't you tell me your news?*" he asked while licking his lips, hungry for a guinea pig sandwich.

"Not a chance!" Sandy glared into Rex's eyes. "NNN— N—Not a chance!" Sandy desperately wanted to prove to Jake and Alexa what a good detective she was, so she wasn't about to give Rex the information about Mrs. Smythe escaping from prison.

"*All right!*" snapped back Rex as he crept away. "*Have it your way. But eventually, I'll find out—I always do!*"

The raven-haired lady opened up her arms and gave the children a big old hug. "Well, Inspector Moustachio and Inspector Girl, what a pretty pleasure it is for—*YOU* to finally meet—*ME*," she said with a grin. "I'm Miss Sally-Mae McGraw, and welcome to the Giddy Goat Ranch."

"How do you know who we are?" asked Alexa.

"Well, you pretty little thing," answered Miss Sally-Mae, "those two old goats hanging by the front door over there told me all about you, of course. They know everything there is to know in these parts. All the mounted animal heads on this side of the magnifying glass talk to each other through the walls that their heads are hanging from. It's so annoying. They spend all day long sending animal e-mail in their heads back and forth to each other. You can't have an eyelash out of place without those two nags getting under your nose."

Miss Sally-Mae bent down to Alexa and adjusted the ribbon in her hair. "That's better," she said, "much prettier. Why, I always tell my little pig, Magnolia, 'Maggie,' that's what I call her, 'a lady must always look her best at all times.' Why, you never know when a blue ribbon day will just pop right up out of nowhere! And everyone knows I just *LOVE* a blue ribbon day!"

CHAPTER EIGHT

Little Magnolia

Magnolia came waddling out of the barn, oinking all the way. She was wearing a pink ballerina tutu with her own shiny tiara perched on top of her wrinkly, pink-skinned head. The blue ribbon she won at the county fair's Miss Piggly Wiggly Beauty Pageant was proudly dangling from her chubby, thick neck.

"That's not a little lady," smirked Rex. *"That's a big old hog."*

"Hush up, Rex," scolded Alexa. "Beauty is in the eye of the beholder."

"Well, this is one eye that just can't stomach looking at such an ugly, pink pig," he shuddered, covering his eyes with his paws in disgust. *"I think I'm going to be sick."*

"Don't be ridiculous, Rex," said Jake. "She's just a pig. A very strange-looking pig, I admit, but still just a pig."

"She's not strange looking at all, silly boy," snapped Miss Sally-Mae. "Magnolia's the most prized of all pigs. Aren't you precious?"

"Ofway oursecay iway amway!" snorted Magnolia.

The children looked baffled and confused at what came out of Magnolia's snout.

"What did she say?" questioned Alexa.

"She said, 'of course I am,' " explained Miss Sally-Mae.

"What type of crazy talk is that?" snickered Rex as he

sniffed around Magnolia with keen, cat-like curiosity.

"Maggie speaks the language of all pigs," announced Miss Sally-Mae.

"And that would be—?" asked Jake.

"Why, Pig Latin, of course!" said Sally-Mae. "And you call yourself a detective? Everyone knows that!"

Rex ran right over to Sandy, looked straight into her teeny-tiny brown eyes with a sly grin, "*Hey, pig face, why don't you speak Pig Latin?*"

Sandy's face got redder than a fire engine when she exploded, "I—AM NOT A PIG, YOU CLOD! I—AM A GUINEA PIG from PERU! Yeah—that's right—Peru. I remembered that this time."

"Rex," scolded Jake. "Play nice."

Alexa immediately went rummaging through her Inspector Girl backpack for a dictionary. "Oh, yes," she shouted, "there it is!" Alexa wasted no time looking up the definition for Pig Latin and read it aloud to the group. "Pig Latin," she defined, "an encrypted, coded form of communication where the first letter of a word is moved behind the last letter of a word with the letters 'ay' added then to the end of the word. Words that start with a vowel are coded in Pig Latin by just adding 'way' to the end of that word."

"So, Rex," Jake surmised, "your name in Pig Latin would be **Exray**."

"That's right, Inspector!" agreed Alexa as she packed away her dictionary. You take the **R** off the front of Rex's name, move it to the end, and then add **ay** to the back and you get **Exray!**"

"*Well then,*" smirked Rex, "***I'mway arvingstay.***

Iway eednay away ancay ofway unatay, andway I'mway oinggay otay eednay ymay itterlay oxbay ealray oonsay!"

"What did you say, Rex?" asked Alexa, jumping up and down in anticipation.

Sally-Mae, knowing all about this crazy language, boasted in a huff, "He just spewed a bunch of babble. He can't speak Pig Latin! It's an acquired tongue of speech only able to be spoken by the most intelligent person or animal."

"Hey, you over-aged beauty queen, I resemble that remark!" yelled Rex.

"Rex, be nice," scolded Jake. "And it's 'resent,' not 'resemble.' When are you going to get that straight?"

Jake then began to search the area for any more clues to the whereabouts of Big Daddy's cows. *He knew the tiara they found in Big Daddy's barn must belong to either Miss Sally-Mae or Magnolia. The goat bell they stumbled upon with the magnolia flower on it clearly came from the Giddy Goat Ranch. And the yellow hay points to the culprit being right in this pink barn. But where could all the cows be hidden, he wondered?* As he was staring very intensely into the magnifying glass, he moved closer and closer to the open barn doors. Just as he was about to step into the barn, Sally-Mae jumped right in front of him, blocking the entrance. She slammed shut the doors with such a force her tiara went flying off into the wind like a runaway Frisbee.

"I don't think you want to go in there, Inspector!" she cried with a wild look in her crystal-clear, blue eyes.

"Why not?" he asked in a very suspicious voice.

"It's just a silly, old mess in there," she explained.

"Why, I'm embarrassed to say, the place looks messier than this old pig pen."

"Oh, he won't mind!" Alexa said cheerfully as she picked up the tiara and plopped it on top of her head. Her strawberry-blonde hair shined against the sparkle of the tiara's diamonds. "His room looks like a pig pen anyway. It's filled with books, Legos, and all kinds of hunk-a-junk. It's just a mess. Mommy is always telling him to tidy it up!"

"Well," Sally-Mae murmured, "there's nothing in there but old, smelly goat blankets and stuff. Nothing you would be interested in any old way."

"Are you sure about that?" questioned Jake. "Maybe there might be a cow or two sleeping in there?"

Miss Sally-Mae got a very angry look on her face as she scurried over to Alexa, snatching the tiara right off of her head in anger. "I know exactly what you're getting at, Inspector. But I had nothing to do with those missing cows of Big Daddy's," she snapped, returning the tiara to the top of her perfectly combed, raven-colored hair. "What would I do with a bunch of smelly, old cows anyway?"

"With all those cows gone," surmised Jake, "your father would become richer than rich selling all his goat milk."

"True," she said as she combed a knot out of Magnolia's curly tail. "But how would that help me—really? My Daddy's wallet is tighter than a saddle strap on a horse's back. He would never give me any of that money, any old way! He thinks my passion for pig beauty is just silly. He never lets me do anything I want."

"Big Daddy told us he heard you arguing with your father at the auction over opening up a pig grooming parlor," Alexa explained as she reached into her Inspector Girl backpack, pulling out three pink ribbons, handing them one by one to Miss Sally-Mae.

"But what does my desire to make all the pigs in the universe beautiful have to do with those silly, old cows?" Sally-Mae asked, tying each of the pink ribbons ever-so-perfectly on Magnolia's tail.

"Since your father wouldn't give you the money to open up your pig grooming parlor," explained Rex, licking the last bit of mud from the pig pen off his tail, *"maybe you kidnapped the cows to get some ransom money from Big Daddy."*

"Don't be ridiculous, you messy, little feline!" yelled Miss Sally-Mae in a nasty huff. "I don't need anyone else's money to help me open up my pig grooming parlor. I'm going to earn that money fair and square on my own."

"How are you going to do that?" questioned Alexa.

"Maggie and I are making a calendar. That's right, a calendar—The Miss Piggly Wiggly Calendar. Magnolia is going to be the star. I was just about to take her picture in the meadow over there by the wishing well. The sunlight is very flattering to Magnolia's pink skin at this time of day. After I finish taking pretty pictures of Maggie, I'm going to make a fortune selling my calendars. Then I'll have enough money to finish—I mean, start my pig grooming parlor."

"Well, you better hurry. The sky looks like it's getting a little cloudy," announced Jake, suspicious of her story. As Jake was looking into the sky warning Sally-Mae about the fading sunlight, he noticed the same light brown hawk that had flown over his head back at Big Daddy's ranch.

Miss Sally-Mae pulled out a pink leash from her dress pocket in a huff and clipped it to Magnolia's collar. She then tossed her long, flowing, black hair into the wind, gazed up into the sky, and said, "Come, Maggie. We want to get your picture before that silly, old sunlight disappears."

Jake raised his magnifying glass to see the whereabouts of any camera. Noticing there was no camera in sight to take Magnolia's picture, he yelled out across the meadow to Miss Sally-Mae with half a grin, "You do know you need a camera to take a picture—don't you?"

Pretending not to hear him, Sally-Mae continued dragging Magnolia across the meadow in a snit. She passed by Bernardo, who was still crying, offered him a hanky to blow his snout, gave him a pat on the head, and continued towards her destination. As she arrived at the well, she looked back at the children with a devilish smile and whispered to Magnolia, "**Iway opehay eythay evernay indfay osethay arnday owscay!**"

"What did she just say?" asked Alexa.

"*I'm not sure,*" answered Rex, "*but she is so guilty of the crime!*"

Alexa scooped up Sandy from the ground, placed her back into her Inspector Girl backpack, declaring, "She's lying! I think she's the culprit who took the cows, too!"

Jake paced back and forth, kicking up dried dirt with his sneaker, as he proclaimed, "Now, wait a minute, you guys. She's definitely hiding something but I'm not so sure she's guilty."

"*Come on!*" yelled Rex. "*She's crazy. Anyone who wants to make pigs beautiful is nuttier than a can of peanuts. Ooooow, speaking of cans of food, I'm still hungry. Hey, pig face, hand me one of my cans of cat food from the bottom of that backpack.*"

"If you call me pig face one more time, I'm going to throw those cans at your head, one by one," threatened Sandy.

"Nice try, Rex," smirked Jake. "But, for the last time, this is no time for a snack."

"Yeah, Rex, we still have to find the cows," explained Alexa.

"And figure out how to read the map to the ttt—t—treasure," added Sandy.

"Mysteries don't solve themselves," continued Jake. "By the way, Sandy, what was the important news you wanted to tell us?"

Sandy sat there trying ever–so–hard to remember what she needed to say.

"*Well?*" questioned Rex, staring at her with his big, golden eyes. "*We're—waiting!*"

Sandy tried and tried to remember that the evil, cake-poisoning cook from The Museum of Time, Mrs. Smythe, had escaped from prison. "I—just can't remember. I'm sss—s—so sorry, you guys," she chutted in despair.

"It's O.K., sweetie," comforted Alexa. "Maybe it will come to you later."

"*I highly doubt that!*" Rex yawned.

CHAPTER NINE

Popcorn Trouble

Suddenly, a huge explosion erupted from somewhere behind the pink, barn shaking everything around the children like a giant earthquake. Little, white, puffy objects started to fall from the sky on the children's heads, just as though a blizzard was beginning.

"Is that snow?" asked Alexa as she stuck her tongue out to grab onto one of the falling puffs.

"It can't be!" puffed Rex. *"It's not even winter."*

"Weirder things have happened on this side of the magnifying glass!" reminded Jake as he proceeded to stick his tongue out to catch one of the falling puffy objects for himself. "Why, I think it's—it's popcorn?"

"Oh, boy, finally a snack. I'm starving!" Rex shouted gleefully. He gathered up all the popcorn he could with his tiny paws as it fell from the sky and gobbled every kernel he could with sheer delight.

Jake ran around the back of Sally-Mae's pink barn, tossing a few kernels of popcorn into his mouth. He examined the odd darkening of the sky with his magnifying glass and followed a trail of grey, smoky-looking clouds to a field of horses surrounding a bright blue stable. There, again, was that hawk perched menacingly on top of a tall tree just off to the side of the stable.

"Look over there, you guys!" he announced as he

pointed to the stable. The popcorn was being shot right out of the stable's tall stone chimney.

Goats from all over the ranch started gathering around the stable to join the horses in a popcorn snack.

"I just love this popcorn!" squealed Alexa as she plucked a few off her shoulder and handed some to Sandy.

Sandy, sitting ever-so-comfortably in the upper-zippered pocket of Alexa's backpack, gnawed at a large, delicious, puffy piece and chutted, "It's so but, but, but—buttery! A little sticky, too—but, but, but—but buttery!"

Jake looked up the hill at Bernardo who was still sitting on top of the same boulder in the middle of the meadow, crying between every bite of popcorn he plucked off his brown, bristly coat.

"Bernardo," Jake called. "Come on! We're going to investigate that stable over there."

Bernardo wouldn't budge. He shook his head no, let out an enormous sigh, and sunk his head low to the ground, still chewing on his popcorn.

"Oh, just forget about him!" cried Rex. *"He's useless, anyway."*

"Rex, be nice. He's just in love!" explained Alexa.

"I think I'm going to cough up a popcorn-filled fur ball from all this mushy bull loves cow stuff!" he moaned.

"Are you sure you won't come, Bernardo?" yelled out Alexa.

Bernardo nodded his head, yes, he was sure.

"Suit yourself, you overgrown horn head," Rex snickered.

"I guess it's just us then," huffed Jake as he started running up the hill to the blue stable.

Trailing closely behind, Alexa asked, "What do you suppose is in there, Jake?"

Jake raised his left eyebrow and said with a sly grin, "I'm not sure, but my detective skills are telling me that stable and this snowing popcorn have to be connected to the disappearance of Big Daddy's cows."

"Ooooo!" Alexa whispered. "The plot thickens. And this could be a very sticky situation."

"*I'll tell you what a sticky situation is!*" Rex said in disgust. "*This goat doo-doo I just stepped in. Outdoor animals are disgusting, uncivilized, and downright rude. I'm going to tell those stupid goats just what I think of their poor bathroom habits.*"

As Rex stormed off to scold the goats, Jake warned, with a wary look on his face, "I wouldn't do that!"

Paying no attention to Jake's warning, Rex started to argue with a very angry-looking grey and white goat with a black patch around his right eye. He was just waiting to use his very large, pointy, ivory-colored horns in a fight.

Jake noticed, except for the goat arguing with Rex, all the other goats who were munching on the popcorn had goat bells dangling from their necks. This particular goat also had a few shavings of yellow hay stuck in a small notch on his left horn.

Worried, Alexa cautioned, "Rex, did you hear Jake?"

"*What did you say?*" Rex asked as he continued scolding the goat.

Jake yelled back, "I said, I wouldn't do that!"

Rex turned his back on the goat as he asked Jake, "*Why not?*"

"Because goats like to—" said Jake, squinting his eyes in anticipation.

Suddenly, before Jake could finish, the black-patched goat backed up and charged toward Rex.

"—KICK!" warned Jake.

With that said, the goat booted Rex right on his butt-sending him flying high into the air.

Jake, Alexa, and Sandy's eyes grew wider, and their mouths hung open in disbelief as Rex, screaming for help, went shooting past them across the popcorn-filled sky, heading directly toward the roof of the stable. The children closed their eyes as Rex slammed right onto the roof.

"Ohhhh, that's gotta' hurt!" exclaimed Sandy with an enormous smile of satisfaction on her face.

As Jake and Alexa ran rapidly to the stable, Jake spouted, "That annoying fur ball never learns."

Rex's claws from his left paw were barely hanging on to a loose shingle on the highest point of the roof above. *"Get me down!"* he begged. *"The snowing popcorn is making it impossible for me to hang on!"*

"Hold on, Rexy Cat!" shouted Alexa. "Hold on!"

"OOOOH—NOOOO!" he screamed as he lost his grip and slid down from the highest section of the roof, bouncing down to the second level below.

Horrified, they all screamed as Rex slid down the popcorn-filled roof, slamming hard into the tippy-top of the stone chimney. He feverishly tried to grab onto whatever he could. His left paw managed to grab onto a ledge as he sighed in relief from having not fallen into the chimney. He laid there paralyzed, too afraid to make any sudden moves. As the popcorn continued to cover the roof, a kernel fell right on top of his nose. Rex tried and tried to shake off the itching kernel without losing his safe grip, but his itchy nose was unbearable. Letting out an uncontrollable sneeze, he lost his hold and slid right into the chimney, screaming all the way down.

"Hurry, Lexy! Hurry!" shouted Jake as he raced towards the stable's big black doors.

Frantic to rescue Rex, Jake and Alexa knocked, bumped, and stumbled over every goat in their way. "Pardon me! Excuse us! Sorry!" exclaimed Alexa, running into the popcorn-snacking herd of goats.

While Sandy bopped away in Alexa's backpack, the children stormed through the stable doors, hitting a gigantic slippery spill of melted butter on the concrete floor. As the stable doors slammed shut behind them, Jake and Alexa went slipping and sliding across the floor, crashing into a tall, orange barrel of unpopped popcorn kernels that tumbled over them.

"*Help! Help!*" cried Rex.

Trying to stand up and balance themselves on the slippery floor, Jake and Alexa scanned the room for Rex.

"Where are you?" they shouted through the never-ending noise of popping kernels of corn.

"*In here!*" echoed Rex. "*Hurry, I'm drowning in this icky mess! And it's getting hotter!*"

Rex was trapped, bouncing around at the bottom of a large, black, cast iron popcorn kettle. The kettle was cooking in the fireplace, popping Rex alive.

Realizing this, Jake and Alexa slid across the floor as fast as they could to the fireplace.

"What do we do?" Alexa asked, shaking in fear for her

very hot kitty cat's life.

"*Hurry!*" moaned Rex.

Jake quickly grabbed the magnifying glass from his back pocket and frantically searched the room for an off switch. The popcorn was rapidly filling the stable past the children's knees.

"That kettle is really starting to overflow!" he shouted through the flying popcorn. "There has to be an off button somewhere." Jake finally found a silver chained pull switch dangling from the rafters of the stable ceiling. "That must be it!" he exclaimed.

"But Jake," sighed Alexa. "It's too high. We're never going to be able to reach it!"

"*Hurry!*" echoed Rex. "*My beautiful golden red fur is getting covered in this thick goop. Ouch! Ouch! Getting hot! Hot! Hot!— Hot!*"

Jake noticed a thin ledge leading over to the lowest point of the rafters. "Sandy," ordered Jake, "you can climb on the ledge, jump to the chain, and shut off the kettle."

"But how am I going to get up to the ledge?" she questioned.

"I know! I know!" announced Alexa as she rummaged through her Inspector Girl backpack. Digging deep to the bottom, she pulled out an old, wooden sling shot with a huge, worn-out, brown rubber band dangling from the corners.

"Lexy," scolded Jake, "why do you have Grandpa Moustachio's slingshot? That's dangerous and totally inappropriate to be playing with. Why—you could shoot someone's eye out with that thing!"

"Don't be silly. I'm not playing with it!" she explained,

tossing it to him. "My friend, Grace, and I borrowed it from Grandma to do our science project with. We're testing the stretching ability of a rubber band to see how long it takes to snap."

With no time to spare, Jake scooped up Sandy, placed her in the slingshot and aimed her towards the ledge in the ceiling above.

"Now w-w-w-wait just a minute!" she nervously chutted. "That f-f-f-fur ball has been trying to place me between two pieces of bread, smother me in mustard, eat me for lunch, and you want to catapult me way up there to save his scrawny neck? **NNN—N—NO WAY!**"

"Come on, Sandy!" coaxed Jake. "Do it for us!"

"Do it for me!!!!!" begged Alexa as she snuggled her on the tip of her tiny brown nose.

Jake pulled back on the rubber band of the slingshot and said, "Be a hero, Sandy!"

"Ohhhhhhhh, all right," she grumbled.

Jake repositioned his aim on the slingshot with his left arm, pulled Sandy back as far as he could with his right hand, and let her go. Sandy went soaring into the popcorn filled air.

"*Any time now!*" echoed Rex, hopping and popping up and down in the kettle.

Sandy skyrocketed to the top ledge, making a perfect landing. Jake and Alexa jumped for joy.

"Good job, Sandy," Jake cheered. "Now make your way over to the corner and jump onto the chain. Your weight should pull it down enough to shut off the kettle."

"Hurry, sweetie!" Alexa shouted. "Hurry!"

Sandy followed Jake's directions and scurried on the

narrow ledge over to the corner where she took a brave leap onto the suspended chain. She dangled there like a circus trapeze artist high above the big top. Slowly, Sandy started to dangle lower and lower as her weight pulled down on the chain. The chain finally lowered enough to shut off the kettle, stopping the endless popping of popcorn from the firey tomb Rex was trapped in.

Jake and Alexa burrowed through the shoulder high popcorn as fast as they could to pull Rex out of his buttery popcorn predicament. Rex looked like a gigantic popcorn ball.

Covered head to toe in melted butter with mounds of popcorn kernels stuck to his golden fur, he moaned, *"It's about time. I was almost a goner!"*

"What do you mean—it's about time?" grumbled Jake as he and Alexa started to pluck the sticky kernels off of his fur. "If you didn't go messing around with that wild, kicking goat, none of this would have happened in the first place."

Rex covered his eyes with his gooey paws in shame and said, *"Oh—I'm so sorry I did that!"*

"You most definitely should be sorry, Rexy Cat," scolded Alexa as she searched her backpack for his cat comb. "That goat could have killed you!"

"I'm not sorry about that stupid old goat," bellowed Rex. *"He deserved it, **doo-dooing** outdoors—**DISGUSTING!** Hasn't he ever heard of a litter box?"*

Jake looked a little annoyed, raised his left eyebrow, crinkled his nose, and muttered, **"Then, what are you sorry about?"**

"I'm sorry I just covered my eyes with my sticky paws," he explained. *"They're stuck! I can't see— I'm blind!"*

"You're not blind, you crazy, sticky hairball!" yelled Jake. "Hopeless—but not blind!"

Jake and Alexa each grabbed one of Rex's paws and gave a tug.

"Ouch!" he cried. *"Not so hard. What are you trying to do—tear off my arms?"*

"Wow, Jake," said Alexa. "He really is stuck!"

The children tried to let go of Rex's arms without any luck. "That's— just great," shouted Jake. "Now we're stuck to him!"

"Hey! WWW—W—What about me?" chutted Sandy, dangling from the suspended chain. "How am I going to get, ddd—d—down?"

"Hold on, sweetie!" yelled Alexa. "We'll get you down!"

In a fierce tug-of-war, Jake and Alexa pulled back and forth, trying to free themselves.

"This cannot be ordinary butter!" sputtered Alexa as she gave another tug. "It's way too gluey!"

"You're right, little lady," said a voice coming from under the mile-high pile of popcorn. "That ain't no ordinary butter from a cow—it's goat butter!"

"Who said that?" Jake inquired, trying to pull himself free from Rex.

The children watched the large mound of popcorn creep slowly towards them.

"I don't like this," cried Rex.

Suddenly, a skinny, young man with brilliant, orangey-red hair and freckles spread endlessly across his face popped right out from under the popcorn. "Howdy!" he said as he emerged. Jake, Alexa, and Rex followed his yellow-hay cowboy hat, firmly sitting on top of his head, move higher and higher towards the ceiling of the stable as he stood up.

"*Wow!*" gazed Rex. "*I'm going to need two ladders and a step stool to look him straight in the eyes!*"

The young man gently grabbed Sandy from the chain and placed her in the front pocket of his blue denim shirt. "Now, let's see about fixin' you three!" he said as he pulled out a pair of shiny, black, rubber gloves from his back pants pocket. He then placed them on his long thin hands and moved towards the children, "Now, this won't hurt a bit."

"*What do you mean won't hurt?*" screeched Rex, trembling in fear.

"I'm just going to wiggle you three free. This sticky goat butter won't stick to my gloves," he explained. He very cautiously pulled Jake and Alexa's hands free from Rex's arms.

"*Ouch!*" moaned Rex. "*That—hurt! My poor delicate fur is ruined!*"

"Don't be such a crybaby, Rex!" scolded Jake. "You'll grow some new fur back in no time."

"*Ah—Ah, I still can't see!*" Rex complained.

"Now just hold still, my little furry friend," said the young man as he started to pull Rex's paws from his eyes.

"I don't think you're quite as furry as when we started this case," Jake smirked.

"*Very funny!*" he groaned, with his paws still stuck to his eyes.

"Wow!" said the young man. "You really are stuck!"

"*Ya' think?*" stammered Rex.

"Listen, you loony, semi-hairless fur ball," yelled Jake angrily, "we wouldn't be in this predicament if you listened to me about going near that wild goat."

"*Yeah! Yeah! Yeah!*" bellowed Rex. "*We already covered that!*"

The tall, young man held Rex's arms and yanked him all the way up towards the ceiling. He gave Rex a little shake as he went higher and higher over his head. All of a sudden, Rex's paws separated from his eyes as the weight of his furry body pulled downward. Dangling from the young man's hands, Rex dropped down to face the young stranger nose to nose.

"*And you are?*" asked Rex to the tall young man.

"Why I'm—Bob Billy Bob!" he declared.

CHAPTER TEN

Culprit Confusion

Suddenly, the stable doors burst wide open from the enormous weight of the pounds of popcorn pressing against them. Sweeping everyone out the door in an enormous tumbling and twisting swell of popcorn, the snackable wave came to a stop as kernels spread all over the pasture.

A tubby, short man wearing a white suit with a matching white shirt and white, shiny cowboy boots topped off with a white, goat-skinned cowboy hat was stomping all around the pasture mad as mad could be. "Bob Billy Bob!" he howled. "I thought I told you to turn off that darn kettle. Now look at the mess ya' made!"

"I'm sorry, Rufus," confessed Bob Billy Bob as he sat in a puddle of goat butter. "I forgot!"

"What do ya' mean—forgot?" scolded Rufus McGraw.

"Miss Sally-Mae needed a camera to take a picture of Magnolia," explained Bob Billy Bob. "She asked me to fetch it for her before the sunlight disappeared, but I forgot where I put it."

"Son," announced Rufus McGraw, "I think you'd forget where your head was if it wasn't sitting right there on top of your shoulders."

"Wait a minute!" interrupted Jake as he stood up dusting all the popcorn off his magnifying glass. "Aren't you the Bob Billy Bob who's Big Daddy's ranch hand?"

"Yeah," added Alexa as she fixed her popcorn-filled hair. "Aren't you supposed to be working on Big Daddy's barbeque sauce recipe?"

Bob Billy Bob got a startled look on his face, jumped up out of the mess, and shrieked, "Oh no! I forgot!" He then went storming off into the hills running as fast as he could back to Big Daddy's cow ranch. Rufus McGraw's white suit glowed ever-so-brightly against the strange, eerie, grey color of the sky as he went running after Bob Billy Bob. Realizing he would have no luck getting him back to clean up the mess of popcorn, Rufus went ranting and raving madly all around the stable.

Sandy scooted over to Rex with the biggest grin ever and chutted, "You do realize I sss—s—saved your life, you hairy ccc—c—clod!"

Rex smirked with a delicious smile and remarked, "*Well then, I guess I won't slap you between two pieces of bread, smother you with mustard, and have you for lunch. At least not— TODAY!*"

Sandy ran over to Alexa for comfort while Jake whispered into Rex's sticky, butter-filled ear, "Oh Rex—you really do love Sandy. Don't you?"

"*Don't be ridiculous!*" he snapped. "*I was just making pleasant conversation. After all, she did shut off the kettle.*"

"She did more than that," Jake reminded. "She saved your furry, little butt! It was good of you to be nice to her."

"*You know what's really good?*" Rex asked.

"What?" he replied.

"*With her stinky memory, she won't remember any of this in ten minutes or so, anyway! Then I can go back to planning my guinea pig sandwich! I think I'll add pickles!"*

While Alexa scooped up Sandy and placed her into the backpack, she noticed Bob Billy Bob's yellow hay hat still buried in the popcorn. "You forgot your hat!" she yelled out as she grabbed it and waved it in the air.

Bob Billy Bob was way too far gone up the mountain to hear her.

Jake noticed a hole on the back of the cowboy hat as Alexa continued to wave it in the air. "Lexy," he called. "Let me see that!"

Jake examined it very carefully with his magnifying glass. "There's a hole in it!" he said quietly to his sister and Rex.

"So?" yawned Rex.

"What do you mean—so?" snapped back Jake.

"It's just a hole in an ugly, old, yellow-hay cowboy hat," Rex replied.

"It's not just any old hole, you matted mess," announced Jake.

"Oh!" shouted Alexa. "I get it—it's a clue!"

Jake, wide-eyed, whispered, "Not so loud. We don't want Rufus to hear us." Jake knelt down with Rex and Alexa following his lead. "The missing hay from this hat matches some of the hay we found behind that secret pink barn Miss Sally-Mae wouldn't let us into. It's also the same color as the hay in Big Daddy's cow barn. And there were a few strands of this hay on the goat that kicked your butt!"

Alexa unzipped her backpack, "Sandy, sweetie," she said, "grab me the hay we collected."

Sandy scurried about the backpack, popped up, and

said as she handed the hay to Alexa, "Look at the fff—f—funny shape of the sun!"

Jake, Alexa, and Rex were so busy with their investigation, they weren't paying any attention to Sandy or the changes in the sun.

As Jake examined the yellow hay with his magnifying glass he noticed Rex eating off the ground.

"What do ya' know!" proclaimed Rex as he nibbled at the kernels on the ground. *"It—is the same hay."*

"Wait a second!" Jake accused. "You were eating popcorn off the floor at Big Daddy's cow barn, weren't you?"

"And I'm still hungry!" he snapped.

"The missing yellow hay we found may not have completely fallen off the culprit's body or the cows' hides after all. Maybe the yellow hay is from the hole in this hat. That would definitely place Bob Billy Bob here at the Giddy Goat Ranch sometime during the crime."

"But how do you know that?" Rex asked mystified.

"Well, when fresh cut hay hits the air, oxygen causes the cut part to turn a slightly brownish color. That takes exactly seventy-two hours for that oxidation to affect the color of the hay."

"That's exactly the time the cows were kidnapped!" Alexa exclaimed.

"Some of this hay looks oxidized. Its edges are a little brown, matching the color of the cut hay on Bob Billy Bob's hat," added Jake. "I'd bet my magnifying glass those cows are hidden somewhere on this goat ranch. The popcorn that you ate at Big Daddy's barn confirms that the kidnapper had to be either eating popcorn or had popcorn with them at the time of the kidnapping. If there had been any popcorn on the ground before the kidnapping, the cows would have definitely eaten it all up."

"So the popcorn was dropped after the cows left the barn," said Rex, stroking his whiskers. *"Interesting!"*

"Maybe the culprit did one last swoop of the barn to make sure they didn't leave any cows behind," Sandy added. "And then dropped the popcorn."

"But Jake, how do you know the popcorn belonged to Bob Billy Bob?" questioned Alexa as she placed the hay back into her backpack.

"We don't—yet!" he declared. "But how many people pop popcorn out here in the middle of nowhere and wear a yellow hay cowboy hat?"

"So that means Bob Billy Bob is the culprit who took the cows," surmised Alexa.

"And who wants to find the ttt—t—treasure!" chutted Sandy.

"I'm not a hundred percent sure, yet," Jake analyzed, while scratching his head. "We still need to figure out who the goat bell belongs to, and my detective skills are telling me there's more to this crime than just Bob Billy Bob simply kidnapping those darn cows for money."

"Don't forget the stranger at the cow auction wearing that funny, yellow cape with the jagged scar running down the right side of his face," Alexa added while pulling the last bit of popcorn from her hair.

"He had to have overheard Chief Buffalo Hump telling Big Daddy all about the cows and that mysterious treasure map," Jake continued.

"Maybe he's the one!" thought Sandy as she squiggled around Alexa's Inspector Girl backpack.

"But what about him?" questioned Alexa as she pointed over to Rufus McGraw, still stomping and ranting in a fury over the popcorn mess.

"I'm not sure where he fits into all this just yet," answered Jake.

"*Wait—Wait —Wait!*" Rex screamed as he took a huge sniff of air. "*That tiara still makes me think it's Sally-Mae who did it! And that big, old pig probably helped her. I can just smell it!*"

Jake looked down at the pile of goat droppings Rex was standing in and said with a huge grin, "That's not the smell of Miss Sally-Mae's guilt you're sniffing."

Rex finally realized he once again was standing in a pile of doo-doo and became as mad as mad could be. His fur puffed up like an overstuffed goose down pillow. Rex jumped up on top of a cross-eyed, golden-brown horse grazing on left over popcorn in the fields and ran all the way up the horse's back to stand way up high on the top of his head. Rex's face turned redder than a ripe apple ready to fall off a tree. He then took one infuriated gasp of air, waved his sticky, matted paws towards the sky, and yelled as loud as could be, "**Hasn't anybody—ever heard—of a litter box!**"

His voice echoed miles and miles into the hills. There was dead silence. Not a chirp of a bird or the buzz of a bee could be heard. All the hundreds of goats and horses stopped eating and stared at Rex, too afraid to move. Rex angrily glared out into the fields and noticed one lonely, disheveled, scrawny, white goat with a twisted horn shaking in fear.

"**You!**" he bellowed to the goat. "**Yeah—I'm talking to you!**"

The scrawny goat fearfully turned away pretending not to have heard Rex.

*"**Have you ever heard of a litter box?**"* Rex questioned wildly. *"**I ask any of you, have you—ever?**"*

The distorted horned goat looked back at Rex with a blank stare and murmured under his breath, "**Naaah!**"

"What did you say?" Rex asked disgusted.

One by one, all the horses and goats that could be seen and heard for miles and miles answered Rex with a naaah, a neigh, another naaah, and yet some more neighs.

Sandy popped her head out and asked, "DDD—D—Does all that mean no?"

Fearful for Sandy's life from Rex's rage, Alexa quickly signaled yes and quickly zipped her up in the backpack for her own good.

Rex, exasperated from his ordeal, collapsed on the horse's head and uttered in despair, *"I'm surrounded by undomesticated morons."* He then slid down the nose of the golden brown horse looking him straight in his big, brown, crossed eyes and whimpered, *"Like I said, surrounded by— morons."*

Rufus McGraw snatched Rex from the tip of the horse's nose, flung him over his shoulder, and said, "Come on little fella', we'll get y'all cleaned up," he announced. "I got a big, old wash bucket back at the house. We'd best get a roof over our heads, anyway. Looks like a storm might be brewing. Why, I don't think I've ever seen the skies this color before. It's almost down-right spooky how everything looks grey out here. After I give ya' a good old scrubbing, ya'll feel like a new man—I mean pussycat."

As he carried Rex off, he yelled out to the children,

"Oh, yeah, Inspector and Inspector Girl, you might want to come along, too! I'm sure you have plenty of questions to ask me about those missing cows."

Jake was anxious to ask Rufus many questions about the crime, but his attention was diverted once again by that same light brown hawk still perched high up in that tree, glaring down upon them.

"Come on, Jake," Alexa called out. "Hurry up!"

"I'm coming," he yelled as he ran to catch up with Alexa. "So—" he asked inquisitively of Rufus, "how do you know who we are?"

Rex raised his sad, little, bouncing, matted, furry head from his limp, dangling body over Rufus's back and stated, *"Now let me guess—the two old goats hanging on the wall by the front door told you!"*

"Well, of course!" declared Rufus, "They do know everything there is to know in these parts. You can't have an eyelash out of place without those two nags getting under your nose."

CHAPTER ELEVEN

If The Tiara Fits

Jake and Alexa followed Rufus down by his house just around the corner from the Giddy Goat Ranch's pink barn. Alexa plopped Bob Billy Bob's yellow-hay cowboy hat on top of her head for safekeeping and stuck a nicely twisted pony tail right through the back hole.

As they passed the pink barn, Rufus said, "Can you believe the color my Sally-Mae made me paint this thing! Whoever heard of a pink barn! Why, it's an utter disgrace!"

Jake, being the great detective he was, never let a good opportunity pass him by. "I'm sure it's not that bad looking inside," he said with a twinkle in his eye. "Why don't we go take a look?"

He tried once again to get inside that pink barn. But when Jake went to open the big white doors, Rufus McGraw jumped right in front of him, blocking the way. Rex was now squashed between the barn doors and Rufus's back.

"*Can this day get any worse?*" Rex cried in pain.

"Where do you think you're going?" Rufus demanded of Jake.

Startled, Jake answered, "Why I thought we might take a look inside. I've never been inside a pink barn before."

"I'll bet it's beautiful!" added Alexa smiling as she added some shiny lip gloss to her parched lips.

Rufus's face became redder than the inside of a ripe

watermelon. "Ya' can't go in there," he yelled with gusto.

"*Why not?*" Rex squeaked, firmly crushed against the door.

"It's just a big, old mess in there!" declared Rufus as he continued to block the door. "Ya'—can't go in there. It's just not suitable for company."

"Mmmmm," smirked Jake. "So we've heard!"

How odd, Jake thought to himself. Sally-Mae said the exact same thing. Could Rufus and his daughter be in this caper together? Are the cows somewhere in that barn? But how could they hide that many cows and without a MOO heard for miles? What about Bob Billy Bob and the stranger at the cow auction with the jagged scar that was shaped like the letter M? Could they all know about the map on the hide of one of the cows? And how would any of them ever be able to figure out which cow it was?

"Well, Mr. McGraw," sneered Jake, "maybe we'll come back and take a look at the inside of this beautiful barn another time when you have a moment to clean up your mess!"

"That would be mighty-fine of ya', Inspector," declared Rufus as he scurried them away from the barn towards the front door of his house.

"Do you think he's hiding something, Jake?" whispered Alexa.

"Most definitely," Jake whispered back, "most definitely."

Still hanging around the front door of Rufus's house were those two old goats, the Nanny Goat sisters, Fannie and Annie.

"Well, hello everybody!" greeted Annie to the approaching group.

"And a hello from me to you, too!" added Fannie.

"Hi, I'm SSS—S—Sandy," she chutted from the backpack.

Annie and Fannie got a confused look on their faces as they glared down at her. "Why, yes, dear, we know," said Fannie.

"We just met you a little while ago—don't ya' know?" reminded Annie.

"Did you have an accident dear and hit you head?" asked Fannie as the bell around her neck rang with every word she spoke.

"I don't think so," thought Sandy. "Did I?" she asked Alexa, while scratching her tiny head in utter frustration.

"No, you didn't, sweetie," comforted Alexa as she stroked Sandy's little head. "She tends to forget a few things now and then," explained Alexa to the sisters.

"Oh dear! Oh me! Oh my!" bellowed the nosey goats.

"We have a message for Rufus, don't we sister?" asked Fannie of Annie.

"Why, I do believe we do!" agreed Annie as she shook her head, whacking her vanilla-colored horns on the wood siding of the house.

"Well don't just hang there cackling about it, ya' annoying old goats," yelled Rufus, "What's the darn message?"

"Your wife called!" declared Fannie with a very long pause.

"AND?" screamed Rufus, stomping all around the doorway.

"She said she'll be back tomorrow from Tatterville," said Annie.

"Her mother's feeling much better," added Fannie.

"Oh, no," groaned Rufus as he carried Rex into the house with the children lagging behind.

"What's the matter?" asked Alexa.

"I lost something of my wife's a couple of days ago," said Rufus. "She's going to be fit to be tied if I don't find it before she gets back. She's not one to make angry!"

"Maybe I can help," offered Jake. "After all—I am the world's greatest detective."

"And a modest one, too!" snickered Alexa as she rolled her eyes.

"No, thanks!" he barked out. "I lost it. I'll find it!"

Rufus ran off into the kitchen to wash Rex up. This gave Jake and Alexa time to investigate his house without him noticing.

Jake took out his magnifying glass and searched the room they were in, looking for any clues. It was a sprawling ranch house completely decorated in a western style. There were deer antler chandeliers, cow-hide rugs, rodeo rope hanging from the walls, and even stuffed animals scattered about.

"Look at that rug, Sandy," gushed Alexa. "Isn't it beautiful? It's an antique. It must be priceless."

"It's ppp—p—pretty," she replied.

"What's this?" Jake questioned as he came upon a gigantic redwood display case.

"Wow," they both whispered, staring at the enormous wall of trophies, ribbons, awards, pictures, and rows of **tiaras**.

Sandy pushed her head out further from Alexa's Inspector Girl Backpack to get a good look for herself. "WWW—W—Wow," she chutted.

The children started examining all the meticulously displayed knick-knacks on the seemingly endless wall, searching for clues.

"I wouldn't do that!" exclaimed a mounted buffalo head hanging from the wall on the other side of the room.

"Why not?" questioned Jake.

"Daisy-Mae, Rufus's wife, doesn't like anyone touching her beauty pageant awards," said the buffalo. "She'll have your head for that! How do you think I wound up here?"

"I see your point." Jake answered. As he started to put everything they had touched back in its original spot, Jake noticed each tiara was hung in the case by a copper hook, and he further noticed one empty hook. "Look, Lexy," he announced, with a suspicious look in his eye. "One of the tiaras is missing!"

"And I know exactly which tiara belongs there," she whispered as she handed him a picture of Rufus's wife, Daisy-Mae.

"I don't believe it!" he said with a chuckle. Jake looked down at the picture of Daisy-Mae. In the picture, she was wearing a diamond-studded tiara with a black, metallic-looking pearl mounted in the center just like the one they found in Big Daddy's cow barn. "Sandy," he asked, "grab me the tiara we found."

Sandy dove to the bottom of the backpack and dragged up the tiara and held it up with all her might for them to see.

Jake knew immediately they had Daisy-Mae's tiara.

But how did it get into Big Daddy's barn? When, and by whom?

"Nice tiara!" noticed the mounted buffalo head.

"What tiara?" Jake snapped back as he stood in front of Alexa, hiding the backpack, Sandy, and the tiara from his view.

"Daisy-Mae's tiara, the one you have hidden in that pink and purple backpack," the buffalo head added with a smirk and a very wet laugh. "Don't worry, *I won't tell*. Six long years ago, I was passing through this very same room, and I made the big mistake of trying on one of her tiaras."

"Why would you, a strong looking buffalo, be wearing a diamond studded tiara?" questioned Alexa with a puzzled gaze across her face.

"Hey," the buffalo explained, "I have my moments."

"Well—I guess a buffalo's gotta' do what a buffalo's gotta' do!" declared Jake.

"Anyway," continued the buffalo, "when she found out, off went my head. I've been hanging here ever since. No one messes with Daisy-Mae. She's an awful woman, drop dead gorgeous, but evil beyond belief. She deserves every bad thing that comes her way."

The children nearly jumped out of their shoes when Rufus sprang into the room, unannounced.

"Well, that's done," he explained, approaching the children. "The cat's drying off, and he'll be out in a minute."

Jake quickly pushed the tiara and Sandy along with it to the bottom of the backpack and out of Rufus's view.

"Your wife sure has a lot of trophies," Jake commented.

"She sure does," replied Rufus. "Why, my Sally-Mae takes right after her Mama. My wife, Daisy-Mae, has won more beauty pageants then any other gal in the county. She hasn't aged a day since I met her. Why I think she might even look a little younger!"

"Where is your wife?" asked Alexa as she ran her hand across the magnificent soft silk of the antique rug.

"She's been in Tatterville for three days visiting her sick mother," he answered nervously.

"Where were you the night Big Daddy's cows were kidnapped?" Jake questioned, scoping out the room with his magnifying glass for any more clues or unusual animals.

"I don't like what you're implying son," scolded Rufus with a scowl on his face.

"Well, with all those cows suddenly gone, your goat milk and butter sales must be better than ever!" stated Jake.

"True!" declared Rufus laughing himself silly, "I've made more money in the last three days than I have made in the last five years. My wife is so happy with all this new found money, she can barely contain herself. She's a woman who likes the finer things in life—ya' know. And once I've perfected my goat butter formula, Giddy Goat Popcorn is going to be bigger then any cow butter-coated popcorn could be. We're going to be richer than our wildest dreams!"

"Then you must be thrilled those cows are gone?" Alexa asked.

"Ya' got that right, but that doesn't mean I took 'em," he snarled with a devilish smile. "I was nowhere near Big Daddy's that night. I was driving my Daisy-Mae to her mother's in Tatterville. You can ask her yourself when she returns tomorrow."

As Jake placed his magnifying glass securely in his back pocket, he declared with suspicion in his voice, "I just might do that!"

Rex came sliding out of the kitchen freshly washed and clean as a whistle. *"Do I not look handsome!"* he announced. *"Why, I feel like a brand new pussycat. Look at my coat. Have you ever seen fur this shiny? I ask you—have you ever?"*

"You look fabulous, Rex!" confirmed Alexa.

"Well, he should," Rufus declared. "I used Honey Hog Honey Body Wash on him. Just look at that fur gleam."

"You know," added Rex, *"Rufus had that bath water waiting for me—ready to go! Wasn't that nice?"*

"Well, not exactly little fella'," Rufus confessed. "Sally-Mae gave Magnolia her morning bath in that wash bucket this very morning. It's a good thing she didn't dump the water out."

Rex just stood there in shock. One lonely tear escaped from the corner of his golden left eye, falling to the floor below his perfectly groomed front legs. It was all he could do to hold back the tears as he started to choke on his emotions. *"You mean you, washed me in used **pig water!**"* he cried as he fell to the floor in a panic.

"Sorry, little man," said Rufus. "I didn't think it would be a problem. You're both animals. Aren't ya'?"

Rex collapsed onto the floor, slammed his paw against the rug and cried, *"I'm a domesticated pet of the highest breed. I am not a cat that washes in used **pig sweat!**"*

Rex was so upset he started gagging and choking.

"Oh, no!" shouted Jake. "Stand back, it's not going to be pretty."

"What's he doing?" yelled Rufus, stomping around the room in a fearful panic.

"Whenever he gets really, really, really upset, he coughs up a mean-looking fur ball," explained Alexa as her big blue eyes grew bigger and bigger in anticipation of the mess.

"And this one's going to be a ddd—d—doooozy," Sandy nodded, poking her head far out from the backpack so she wouldn't miss a single moment of what was about to happen.

"Rex," Jake warned, "not on that rug!"

Rex was gagging and choking as he tried to clear his throat and stop the explosion, but it was too late. Out came the largest fur ball the children had ever seen, popcorn and all.

"Noooooooo!" Rufus bellowed. "Not on Daisy-Mae's great-grandma's rug. She's not going to like this a bit!"

Jake and Alexa just stood there in shock.

"Maybe his head will be mounted on the wall next!" bellowed the buffalo.

"*Well, I feel much better!*" burped Rex with a satisfied look on his face.

Trembling madly, Rufus slowly sat down on his favorite goat-hide chair and cried, "Daisy-Mae is going to be madder than a turkey on Thanksgiving!"

"Well, then," announced Jake pushing his way closer to the door. "I guess it's time to go! Yep, definitely time to go!"

"That sounds good to me!" Alexa added as she dragged her backpack and Rex towards the door.

"Thanks—ah—for your—ah—hospitality," Jake mumbled as they fled the house. "See ya' later!"

They ran for their lives through the front doorway zooming passed the Nanny Goat sisters.

"Oh, dear!" exclaimed Fannie. "What's your rush?"

"How rude!" uttered Annie. "Imagine, not even a good-bye!"

Sandy stuck her head out from the backpack, looking back at the nosey goat sisters, as Alexa ran as fast as she could to catch up with Jake and Rex. "Hi," yelled Sandy to the sisters. "My name's—Sandy!"

"That poor little thing," sighed Annie, shaking her head.

"She can't remember a darn thing," stated Fannie as she jingled her bell.

"Not now, sweetie," Alexa shouted in all the chaos. She then pushed Sandy's little brown head down into the backpack and quickly zipped her up so she wouldn't fall out.

"We need to get out of here," warned Jake, running as fast as he could up the mountain. "Rufus is so mad there's no telling what he may do."

"Not to mention what he'll do when he finds out we have his wife's tiara," Alexa breathlessly added.

"Yeah," huffed Jake, "that buffalo better keep his mouth shut!"

"*What buffalo?*" hissed Rex, sprinting through the grass. "*Whose tiara do we have?*"

Jake could barely catch his breath he was running so fast. "We'll fill you in later," he said to Rex.

"*I just can't believe this,*" Rex snapped, "*I take a short bubble bath, and I miss all the action!*"

"I think the real action is just about to begin!" exclaimed Jake.

Frantic to find Bernardo, Rex, Jake, and Alexa knocked,

bumped and stumbled into every goat in their way. "Pardon me! Excuse us! Sorry!" they exclaimed. There he was, still sitting on that same old boulder crying his eyes out.

"Bernardo," Jake hollered out. "We're leaving!"

Bernardo just sat there, not moving an inch of his bristly, brown fur. Panicking, Jake thought fast of a way to get Bernardo off his butt.

"Bernardo, the cows are at Big Daddy's," he yelled.

"**COWS!**" Bernardo bellowed.

"That's right," Alexa screamed, exhausted from running—**THE COWS!**"

Bernardo leaped up from the boulder, took a deep breath, wiped some of the tears away from his eyes, and stampeded towards the children. He swooshed frantically passed Sally-Mae who was about to take a picture of Magnolia. The force of his gallop spun them around, knocking her and Magnolia right down to the ground, screaming in terror. Bernardo made his way to the children, scooped them all up onto his back, and fled headlong in a panic out the broken gates of the Giddy Goat Ranch towards home.

CHAPTER TWELVE

The Great Escape

Bernardo forged ahead, frantically racing down the river towards Big Daddy's ranch. The steam from his nose sailed across the unexpectedly hazy, grey-colored landscape with each gallop he took. Jake and Alexa bounced up and down on his back as they filled Rex in on what he missed while he was taking his bath.

"*So the tiara belongs to Daisy-Mae,*" Rex said, springing up and down. "*So who took the cows, then?*" he asked.

"I think Bob Billy Bob took the cows and planted the tiara in Big Daddy's barn to make it look like Daisy-Mae did it!" Alexa stated as she adjusted the yellow-hay hat firmly on her head.

"I'm not so sure about that, Lexy," replied Jake.

"*But you said Daisy-Mae was at her mother's,*" said Rex.

"So—Rufus said!" Jake admitted, holding tightly onto Bernardo's bristly coat. "We don't know that for sure. She could be hiding out somewhere with those cows right now guilty of the crime!"

"But Bob Billy Bob definitely needs money, and the hay we found from this hat definitely places him at the pink barn," said Alexa.

"Well, that is ttt—t—true, Jake," added Sandy.

"And we know those cows are hidden in there

somewhere," mentioned Alexa. "Plus the popcorn he was making at the stable definitely connects him to the popcorn that Rex ate back at Big Daddy's cow barn."

"*No-No-No!*" announced Rex. "*Sally-Mae kidnapped those stupid cows. She must have overheard Chief Buffalo Hump telling Big Daddy at the auction about the treasure and figured out if she stole the cows and uncovered the map she would have enough money to build that stinky pig beauty parlor. I'll bet Magnolia helped her and was wearing Daisy-Mae's tiara the whole time.*"

"But what about the goat bell we found?" Sandy asked.

"Well," said Jake, "you all have a point. But my detective skills are telling me Rufus took those cows and is connected to the tiara, the goat bell, the hat, and the popcorn Rex ate. He had the perfect motive. If he got rid of all those cows, his goat milk and goat butter-covered popcorn would make him richer beyond his wildest dreams."

"*You can't argue with that!*" Rex exclaimed.

"True," replied Alexa, "but he didn't have the opportunity! You heard him; he was taking his wife to her mother's in Tatterville when the cows were stolen."

"We don't know that for sure, either" added in Jake with a wrinkle in his forehead as his eyebrows rose in a deep thought.

"*The Inspector's gotta' point!*" Rex smirked.

"And, at this point in the investigation, any one of them could actually be guilty," declared Jake. "There are still a few missing pieces to this puzzle."

"*Yeah,*" added Rex as he looked up at the odd-looking sky. "*And once we find them, the culprit will be as clear as that hawk soaring past the sun, which, by the way—looks a little funny. Doesn't it?"*

"What hawk?" shouted the children.

They all took a good look up into the eerie, grey-colored sky, and finally noticed the eclipsed half shape of the sun as the moon started its journey to block its light. The light-brown hawk squawked endlessly as it majestically glided into the warmth of the partially covered sun.

Suddenly, Jake heard a mumbling from the magnifying glass as it vibrated in his back pocket. "Inspector!" muttered the voice.

Alexa curiously raised her eyebrow and announced, "Ah, Jake, your pants are talking."

"Inspector Moustachio!" shouted the voice again.

Jake quickly moved his attention away from the solar eclipse and the hawk to grab his magnifying glass swiftly from his back pocket. To his complete and utter shock, it was Delbert, The Keeper of Time.

"Hi, Delbert, what's up?" Jake asked.

Delbert had a very serious look across his wrinkly face. His blue-grey moustache twitched in fear. "Inspector," he stuttered, "I have horrible news. The evil Baron Von Snodgrass has helped Mrs. Smythe escape from jail!"

"*Escaped!*" cried Rex, bouncing all about Bernardo's back. Rex frantically ripped the magnifying glass out of Jake's hand. Shaking as he held it, he stared into Delbert's worried eyes and shouted, "*What do you mean escaped?*"

An annoyed look spread across Jake's face as he demanded, "Give me that, you pesky hairball!" Jake grabbed the magnifying glass back, eager to hear Delbert's answer.

Delbert started to explain that Mrs. Smythe was being carefully watched by Gerard the Giraffe, who's the mounted guard on the prison wall. While she was baking lemon tarts for the other prisoners, an enormous bolt of lightning exploded, and a huge vortex of wind started to blow right there, inside the prison. Then, from out of thin air, an evil-looking man with an odd-shaped scar running through his tiny black moustache appeared from the tunnel of wind. He took Mrs. Smythe by the hand and led her into the vortex of wind to escape. But not before she viciously tied poor old Gerard's extra-long neck into a gigantic knot to prevent him from telling anyone what had happened.

Shocked and speechless, Jake, Alexa, and Rex just sat there with their eyes and mouths wide open. It was all they could do to keep from falling off Bernardo as he stomped his way towards home.

"I fear after all this time he will come after you, Inspector," announced Delbert. "Baron Von Snodgrass and his henchmen will stop at nothing to get your magnifying glass. Possessing one magnifying glass gives you both great powers. But he who possesses both magnifying glasses will have the power to unravel the mysteries of the universe and unleash a power beyond cataclysmic proportions. Snodgrass craves that power! You're in grave danger!"

"*Danger?*" screamed Rex as he wrestled the magnifying glass out of Jake's hand again. "*What do you mean danger?*"

Exasperated, Jake snatched the magnifying glass back. "DD—Delbert," stuttered Jake as one hand trembled, holding up the magnifying glass, while the other held tightly onto Bernardo's thick fur. "You wouldn't happen to know the shape of his scar—would you?"

"Gerard said it was shaped like an—*M*!" answered

Delbert. "A very jagged-looking, *M*."

"*M?*" shouted Rex as he went to grab the magnifying glass. "*What do you mean, M?*"

Jake stared down at Rex with an annoyed look in his eye. "Touch my magnifying glass one more time," he warned, "and you're going to be sleeping at the dog pound whenever we get home!"

Rex had a very sheepish look on his furry face as he declared, "*You're the boss!*"

Jake, immediately realizing Snodgrass was the stranger at the auction, asked, "What should I do?"

"The power is in you, Inspector, to defeat Snodgrass," explained Delbert. "You are the one who is purest of heart and thought," he continued. "I just know it!"

"But how do you know?" asked Alexa with a worried frown.

"Because you, Jake, are the grandson of the famous Inspector Buck Moustachio and the great-great-grandson of the first Inspector Jake Moustachio. It's your *DESTINY!*"

"But remember, Inspector," Delbert warned, "Snodgrass has had a lifetime to master the powers within his magnifying glass. You will have to be quick to learn the powers of yours if you are ever to defeat him and gain control of his magnifying glass!"

"But how?" uttered Jake.

"Your magnifying glass and you are one," Delbert explained. "The power within you controls the power within the magnifying glass. Master your mind and thoughts and you will be able to learn how to control the magnifying glass."

"You make it sound so simple," replied Jake.

"If you are the one," declared Delbert, "it will be! If you

can defeat Snodgrass and gain control of his magnifying glass, the mysteries of the universe will await you. Good luck, Inspector. Good luck to you all!"

Jake thanked Delbert, and they all said goodbye. Delbert quickly vanished from the magnifying glass as Jake held it tightly in the palm of his hand.

Jake took a deep breath, mustered up his bravery, tucked the magnifying glass into his back pocket, and stuttered anxiously, "I—I can do this. Can't I?"

"Inspector Girl will be by your side all the way," declared Alexa as she patted him on his back.

"And don't forget everyone's favorite Critter Detective, Me!" Rex exclaimed with a big comforting grin.

"And mmm—m—me, too!" chutted Sandy, from atop Alexa's backpack.

Rex glared at Sandy and snapped, *"Hey, pig breath. How come you don't look as surprised about Mrs. Smythe escaping from prison and fleeing with the evil Baron Von Snodgrass as the rest of us are?"*

Sandy stared at Rex, dazed and confused, not sure what exactly to say. As Delbert was giving them the awful news, she remembered the Nanny Goat sisters informing her of the exact same thing.

"Well?" snarled Rex, licking his lips in anticipation of a pig sandwich.

Sandy, frozen in fear, just shook there in Alexa's Inspector Girl backpack too afraid to speak.

"What's the matter, sweetie?" Alexa asked as she picked her up. "Why are you trembling?"

Sandy gasped a tiny bit of the hazy air and blurted out, "I'm sss—s—sorry. Those two goat sisters told me all about that evil cook escaping from jail back at the goat ranch. I tried and tried to tell you, but no one would pay attention to me. Jake was bbb—b—busy looking for clues and you were waiting for that pig lady to come out of her pink barn. And Rex, well he just wanted to be a better detective than me and have me for lunch. I—I—forgot. You know I have a problem remembering stuff—don't ya'?"

"Now, let me get this straight—," growled Rex as he sprang up and down on Bernardo's back. *"You've known all along that crazy, cake-poisoning cook escaped with that wicked baron. What's the matter with you? Why don't you get some mustard, smother yourself with it, slide between two pieces of bread, add a pickle, so I can finish you off and put myself out of my misery!"*

"Rex," scolded Jake.

"It's O.K., sweetie. We understand," consoled Alexa as she gave Rex an annoyed look while caressing the shaking Sandy under her tiny, furry chin. "Don't we, Rex?"

"No, I don't understand!" exclaimed Rex, ranting and raving on Bernardo's back. *"Snodgrass has been here all along. He was at the auction. Hello—anybody listening? The stranger with the* **M**-*shaped scar on his face! Why, I'll bet any minute his henchmen will be coming to wipe us out."*

Riding along on Bernardo's back, Rex, Alexa, and Jake started arguing about the predicament they were in.

"No matter what," Jake proclaimed, "we have to finish this case."

"No way!" shrieked Rex. *"We have to go home!"*

"I agree with Jake! We stay and finish the job." declared Alexa as she adjusted the cowboy hat on her head to keep it from falling off from the bouncy ride.

"*Why do I feel this is not going to end wel?*" groaned Rex.

Sandy nervously scurried about the top of Alexa's backpack, trying not to get dragged into the argument. She turned her little head towards the grey-colored hills behind them and noticed in the distance, three dangerous looking men fast approaching on horseback. "GGG—G—Guys!" she warned. As usual, she thought, no one was paying any attention to her. Once again, she warned, "Hey you ggg—g—guys!" Jake, Alexa, and Rex were so busy arguing with each other they still didn't hear her. Exasperated, she climbed to the bottom of the backpack to look for something that would get their attention. Sandy found a set of brass cymbals, feverishly dragged them to the top and slammed them together with all her might.

Startled from the enormously loud bang, Bernardo stopped dead in his tracks and started crying like a baby again. The loud noise of the cymbals left a deafening ring in his ears. As they all stared at her with blank looks on their faces, she stood up with a satisfied grin, pointed towards the three men, and said, "NNN—N—Now do I have your attention?"

"*Like I said,*" moaned Rex as he stared off into the distance, shaking like a leaf on a windy fall day, "*this is not going to end well—is it!*"

Panicking, Alexa whispered into Jake's ear, "Is this the

part where the bad guys come after us?"

"I'm afraid so," he answered back in a frightful tone.

Frozen still, she asked, "Should I be afraid?"

"Very," Jake warned.

Suddenly, Alexa's face became redder than her hair as she let out the most terrifying of screams that echoed far, far into the hills.

Rex's rusty-colored fur puffed up in terror as he cried, *"We're doomed! Doomed I say! As doomed as doomed can be!"*

Yelling through Alexa's screams, Jake exclaimed, "For once, I agree with you! We need to get out of here."

Jake grabbed onto Bernardo's horns yelling giddy up, giddy up, but he would not budge. "Bernardo, we have to go," he warned. "We really have to go!"

They all started yelling and screaming at Bernardo to move, but the ringing in his ears from the cymbals smashing together prevented him from hearing them.

Rex jumped off his back, ran around to the front and faced him square in the eyes. *"Move it, you overgrown bully!"* he ordered as he pulled on his brass nose ring.

"Hurry, Jake," shrieked Alexa. "They're getting closer."

Jake was trying as hard as he could to think of a way to escape their impending doom, but with no luck.

Frustrated, Rex ran around to Bernardo's back and shouted, *"Desperate times call for desperate measures."* He grabbed onto Bernardo's tail with his right paw, swung his left paw into the hazy-grey, eclipsed sky, and released his sharp cat claws.

"Desperate times call for desperate measures," confirmed Jake as he gave Rex the signal.

"*Hold on,*" warned Rex, giving Bernardo a very sharp claw slap on his butt.

Bernardo let out a painful cry and took off like a torpedo down the river as Rex, dangling from his tail, hung on for dear life.

CHAPTER THIRTEEN

Cat Food To The Rescue

As the moon slowly eclipsed over the sun, Bernardo galloped madly away with all his strength as the three henchmen got closer and closer in hot pursuit.

The force of the wind was so powerful, Bob Billy Bob's yellow-hay hat flew right off Alexa's head into the wind and plopped right on top of Rex, covering his furry face. "They're gaining on us, Jake," she proclaimed.

"*What's going on? I can't see anything!*" exclaimed Rex, through the blustery wind as he swung all around, hanging onto Bernardo's tail.

"Try taking the hat off, you pesky pet," screamed Jake as he tried to steer Bernardo's horns to the right and then to the left.

"*Oh, that's better!*" exclaimed Rex as he threw it into the wind.

"Are you insane?" Jake scolded, bouncing all around. "You just tossed a perfectly good clue away."

"*Well, you told me to get rid of the hat,*" sighed Rex. "*Didn't ya'?*"

"I told you to take it off, you fur brain, not throw it into the wind."

"Who are those ggg—g—guys chasing us?" chutted Sandy nervously, looking behind them.

"Well, either that-tiara loving buffalo ratted us out

and told Rufus we have his wife's tiara and those are his henchmen, or Snodgrass has finally found us," guessed Jake.

"Whoever they're working for, they're gaining on us," screamed Alexa as she pointed at them. "We have to do something." Alexa let out another terrifying scream that shook the clouds in the grey, eclipsed sky.

The three men were getting closer and closer to reaching them. They were dastardly looking villains with black bandanas masking their faces. Bernardo was no match for the thoroughbred horses that the henchmen were riding on. He tried and tried to move as fast as he could, but the pain from Rex's sharp claw swat and his endless crying started to slow him down.

In utter dismay, Jake pondered for a solution to the treacherous mess they were in. His eyes grew wide as the masked assailants approached ever so closely behind them. "Lexy, do you still have Grandpa's slingshot?" he asked in a panic.

Alexa rummaged quickly through her backpack and pulled out the old wooden sling shot with the huge, worn out, brown rubber band daggling from its corners and tossed it to Jake.

"Whatever you're planning on doing," she screamed anxiously at the top of her lungs, "now would be a good time!"

"I have an idea," Jake declared with a sparkle in his green eyes. "Do you still have those three cans of cat food we packed for Rex?"

"I think so," she said as she and Sandy feverishly searched the bottom of her Inspector Girl backpack for them.

Alexa whipped out a can and flung it to Jake.

Rex could feel and smell the stinky breaths of the wild, black stallions on the back of his puffed up furry neck as he tried to scamper fast and furiously up Bernardo's tail. Trying not to fall off with every effort he made, he snapped at Jake, *"What do you think you're doing?"*

As fast as he could, Jake placed the can of catfish medley into the slingshot, pulled back on the can and the brown rubber band, and took aim at one of the masked henchmen. "What does it look like I'm doing," muttered Jake. "I'm taking those bad guys out one by one!"

"Not with my catfish medley, you don't!" Rex exclaimed. *"I haven't had my lunch yet!"*

"If we don't get rid of them, we're goners," Alexa hysterically screamed.

"Desperate times call for desperate measures," Jake shouted through the wind as he shot the can of catfish medley across the eclipsed sky, soaring towards the first henchman's head.

"Nooooooo!" cried Rex as he was flung back and forth, still hanging from Bernardo's tail.

A direct hit knocked the masked stranger off his horse, leaving two treacherous villains to deal with. Jake, Alexa, and Sandy screamed for joy while Rex moaned at the loss of his catfish medley.

Alexa grabbed the second can of cat food, turkey with giblets, and threw it to Jake.

"No—No—No," cried Rex, with tears rolling from his sad, round, golden eyes. *"Not the turkey with the giblets—it's my favorite. Golden moist chunks of turkey smothered in gravy with a sprinkle of just the right amount of giblets—I'm starving."*

Alexa and Sandy let out a piercing scream as the second masked man was almost upon them.

Jake swiftly aimed and fired the second can of cat food at the second masked scoundrel, just as he was about to grab them.

The can made a direct hit, clunking the second rascal on the head and knocking him to the dusty ground.

With tears pouring down his face, Rex moaned, *"Not the giblets!"*

"Yes!" shouted Jake with a relieved smile on his face. "Two down—one to go!"

"Parting is such sweet sorrow, 'till I taste you again, fair turkey with giblets," Rex professed, dangling in a stream of wind and dust from Bernardo's stampeding run.

With an irritated look on his face, Jake scolded, "Don't be so dramatic, you whiney fur ball! It's just food."

Flipping and flopping as he swung on Bernardo's tail, Rex asked, *"Why is it every time we get into one of these predicaments, I'm the one that has to suffer?"*

The final henchman was approaching, determined to get them. His deep, black eyes glared with evil as he stared long and deadly at Jake. Finally, his horse reached them, ferociously galloping side by side with Bernardo. His brass nose ring swung in the wind as he snarled back at the black stallion trying to pull ahead of him.

"Hurry, Bernardo, you can do it!" cried Alexa, rummaging for the last can of cat food at the bottom of her backpack. "Sandy, do you see it?" she asked.

"I think sss—s—so," she chutted, diving towards the silver and blue can lying beside Alexa's large bag of multicolored marbles.

With the force of the wind blowing her hair into her face, Alexa could barely see Jake as she grabbed the can and tossed it over to him.

"*Not my tuna surprise,*" moaned Rex.

"**Not now!**" yelled Jake as he loaded the slingshot with the can of tuna surprise. Just as Jake shot the last can, Bernardo jumped over a rock causing the can to misfire and fall to the ground. As the can rolled into the rambling river, the evil-looking masked man galloped on, letting out a wickedly wild laugh. He was getting ready to attack his prey.

Alexa let out yet another horrific scream as she searched without success for another can of cat food. "Isn't there any more?" she wondered.

"*Keep searching sister, but you're not going to find any,*" Rex growled.

With the wind and dust continuously blowing through her hair, she yelled desperately, "Why not?"

Rex got an angry, yet satisfied, look across his whiskers and bellowed, "*Because somebody wouldn't let me take more than three cans on the trip!*"

Remembering there were only three cans, a panicked looked spread across Jake's face. He had to try and figure a way out of this mess.

"*I'll bet you're sorry now—Inspector!*" shrieked Rex. "*If you had let me pack more than three cans of food, we wouldn't still be in this mess! But NOOOOOOOOOO, you only wanted three! Now what are we gonna do?*"

Sandy, trembling, popped her head out from the backpack, looked at the menacing stranger and questioned, "I—I—Is that Snodgrass?"

"I'm not sure," Jake yelled back as he tried to steer Bernardo away from the henchman. "I can't see if he has a scar with that black bandanna covering his face."

"Ahhhhhh!" they all shouted as the evil man tried to nab them.

Sandy felt so bad about forgetting to warn them about Mrs. Smythe escaping from prison with The Baron that she wanted to do something to make it up to them. As the masked assailant put out his hand to try to grab them a second time, Sandy yelled to Jake, "Sh—Sh—Shoot me! Shoot me over!"

"*Yeah,*" added Rex, with a huge smile emerging under his whiskers, "*that's a great idea! We can kill two birds with one stone. We get rid of the bad guy and the pig!*"

"You can't, Sandy," cried Alexa. "Jake, don't do it!"

"Please," Sandy begged. "I need to help. I—I feel just awful about forgetting that Mrs. Smythe escaped with The Baron. Please let me do this?"

Jake snatched Sandy right up and positioned her into the slingshot. He aimed her towards the laughing henchman, pulled back hard on the rubber band, let it go, and proclaimed, "This is soooo against my better judgment!"

Alexa screamed in horror, fearing for Sandy's safety.

Sandy went soaring into the grey-soaked, eclipsed sky. Her short fur blew in the wind as she rocketed towards the racing black stallion and the masked stranger. She landed onto his right hand. Sinking her claws into the supple, shiny, black leather of his glove, she gained her balance and ran ever-so-fast up his arm to the back of his neck and then slipped down his shirt.

Startled, the dastardly henchman momentarily let go of the reins of his horse as he started to wiggle and squirm out of control. Sandy rapidly ran around in and out of his clothes, trying to distract his attention away from the children.

Jake, firmly holding onto Bernardo's horns, guided him over to the out-of-control, black horse and tried to nudge him off balance. Sandy then worked her way up the masked man's back and over his black cowboy hat. She then dangled on the front rim, looking him square in the eyes, gave him a wave hello, and pulled down his black bandanna.

They all gasped in disbelief. There was no scar hidden under his mask. The henchman was not the evil Baron Von Snodgrass after all.

Jake looked up and saw they were headed right for the large weeping willow tree that Big Daddy had rested the eight foot ball of toilet paper against earlier. "Time to go, Sandy!" he exclaimed.

"Hurry, sweetie!" shouted Alexa. "Hurry!"

Sandy fearlessly ran over his hat and down his back. Trying to repeatedly grab her, the unscrupulous man never noticed his out-of-control stallion was headed right for the tree. Jake moved in as closely as he could. Sandy made a gigantic leap, landing right on Rex's head as he still dangled wildly from Bernardo's tail.

"*Get off of me, you stupid pig!*" he squawked.

Sandy jumped off Rex's head, ran straight up Bernardo's tail, and right into the comfort of Alexa's warm, hugging arms.

"You were amazing," she squealed, hugging and kissing her all over her tiny head.

The out-of-control henchman and his horse slammed right into a low hanging branch of the weeping willow tree, knocking themselves both to the ground.

With Bernardo now at top speed, they all cheered in utter delight from their victory.

Suddenly, their cheers were interrupted by a loud rumbling. The ground began to shake beneath them.

"What is that, an earthquake?" questioned Rex.

A gigantic shadow loomed over them as they looked back and saw the huge, eight-foot ball of toilet paper rolling straight for them.

"Ahhhhhh!" they screamed, frozen in fear.

"Faster, Bernardo," coaxed Jake. "Faster!"

The giant ball was rolling down the hill with bits of toilet paper flying out as it increased its speed, threatening to flatten them like pancakes.

"We're doomed!" cried Rex, trying to claw his way up Bernardo's tail. *"Doomed, I tell ya'!"*

Racing towards Big Daddy's cow grazing field, Bernardo made an enormous leap over the white fence. They all went flying into the air plopping down haphazardly onto Bernardo's back as he hit the ground with a gigantic thud.

Bernardo came to a breathless, screeching stop in the middle of the grassy field. Hoping the fence would protect them from the rolling ball, they turned and looked back up the hill only to see the gigantic sphere heading straight for the fence. The eight foot super absorbent ball bounced off the fence and flew straight into the sky, eclipsing the moon that was eclipsing the sun. They all screamed in a panic as the shadow from the falling ball came over their heads.

"I agree with Rex," sighed Jake. "We're doomed!"

"Ahhhhhhhhhhhh!" screamed Alexa, Sandy, and Bernardo.

In a quandary, Rex asked himself, "***Why do I feel I'm forgetting something? Now let me see—what was it?***" Rex thought and thought out loud. "***I know I packed my stuffed mouse collection in my toy box—no, that wasn't it. Mmmmm, I added fresh cat litter to my box—no, that wasn't what I forgot. Mmmmm, I just know it's on the tip of my tongue.***"

Jake, once again annoyed by Rex's rambling, desperately yelled, "We're about to be smashed into smithereens, and you're babbling about household chores, you crazy cat!"

A wave of clarity splashed across Rex's face as he remembered what he'd forgotten. Rex sprang up on Bernardo's back, bolted over to Alexa, unzipped the side compartment of her Inspector Girl backpack, and ripped out a super-duper, jumbo can of ocean fish cat food. He quickly ran over to Jake, snatched the slingshot from his front pocket, aimed the can towards the sky, and shot it directly into the center of the falling, deadly ball.

CHAPTER FOURTEEN

That's The Ticket

The direct hit caused the ball to explode over their heads. Yards and yards of toilet paper showered from the sky, cascading over everyone as it floated to the ground.

Buried under the mounds and mounds of toilet paper, Rex popped his fuzzy head out and smirked, *"You really have to get your parents to stop buying toilet paper in bulk!"*

Jake popped his head out next "Did I or did I not say you could only take three cans of cat food," he scolded in a huff. Spitting out some toilet paper from the corner of his mouth, he added, "We shook on it, hand to paw!"

"Well, it's a good thing for you, for all of us, I didn't listen," Rex hissed. *"Now, isn't it?"*

Out from under the toilet paper, Alexa raised her head with Sandy angrily plopped on top. "No wonder my backpack felt a little heavy," announced Alexa. "That was one big can of cat food! And all this time I thought it was heavy because of Sandy."

Sandy was mad as mad could be. "You let me get catapulted over to that masked henchman when you had an extra can of cat food all along, you hairy ccc—c—clod," Sandy grumbled at Rex. "That could have been the end of me!"

"We should be so lucky!" snickered Rex.

"Rex!" Alexa said with a disapproving look. "Naughty—naughty!"

"Hey, why is it when pig breath forgets something, all is forgiven? Need I remind you, she's known all along that crazy cook escaped with that treacherous Baron," declared Rex. *"So—I slipped an extra can of cat food into the backpack. No harm done. Besides, I saved our lives. What did that stupid pig ever do?"*

"She's not a stupid pig," scolded Jake. "She saved our butts back there. If it wasn't for Sandy, that henchman would have done us in. And in case you forgot, she saved your furry butt from getting popped alive in that fired-up kettle back at the stable."

Rex's fluffy, white cheeks became blush-red with shame as he slid his tail between his legs. *"Well,"* he grumbled, *"I guess we're even."*

Hearing all that, Bernardo stood up, crying like a baby.

"Oh—brother! Doesn't he ever stop!" exclaimed Rex, handing Bernardo some toilet paper. *"Here, wipe your eyes and your nose. That dribble on your nose ring is making me sick!"*

With that said, they all burst out laughing as they formed a long-overdue group hug wrapped in yards and yards of super absorbent toilet paper.

Big Daddy came running up the hill with Bob Billy Bob sheepishly following close behind. He had a hopeful look on his big burley face at the prospect of seeing his beloved cows back where they belong. He sprang over the white fence and began throwing toilet paper frantically everywhere. Searching under everyone and everything, he bellowed, "Where are my doggone cows?"

Jake's face became a rosy color of embarrassed red as he answered, "Well, here's the funny thing—we haven't exactly found them yet!"

"What do ya' mean, ya' haven't found 'em yet?" snarled Big Daddy. "I sent ya' up the Red River with Bernardo hours ago!"

Jake thought to himself, gee, that river sounds awfully familiar to me. Where have I heard that before?

"Your secretary said y'all can solve any crime!" Big Daddy argued, glaring down at the young detectives.

In a huff, Jake jumped right back up on Bernardo's back so he could look Big Daddy straight in the eyes. "What secretary?" he asked. "I don't have a secretary."

"Yeah, ya' do!" Big Daddy barked.

"No, I don't!" exclaimed Jake.

Big Daddy shouted back, "Are you calling me a liar, son?"

"*Oh, this is going to get ugly,*" Rex sighed as he dove under the mounds and mounds of toilet paper for cover.

Alexa, Sandy, and Bob Billy Bob just stood there shaking in fear. "I'm sorry, Bob Billy Bob. We lost your yellow-hay hat," whispered Alexa.

"That's O.K., little lady," he said. "I'm always losing that hat anyhow. It'll show up. It always seems to find its way back to my head at some point. "

"When was the last time you lost it?" questioned Jake, in a suspicious tone.

"The day of the auction," he answered. "I was wearing it when we inspected the cows. I took it off to scratch my head, but I forgot where I put it down."

"But you were wearing it when you were at the Giddy Goat Ranch's blue stable," Alexa whispered so Big Daddy wouldn't hear that he was at the ranch earlier.

"Rufus gave it to me," Bob Billy Bob whispered back. "He said it was blowing around in the wind. I can't reckon how it blew all the way over there, though."

Big Daddy was fit to be tied in anger. "Never y'all mind about that stupid darn hat. The Inspector just accused me of lying. Big Daddy ain't no liar. I spoke to your secretary myself after I got your number off your dang business card," he explained.

"What business card?" Jake asked. "We don't have any business cards." Jake gave a perplexed look over to Alexa and Sandy. "Do we?" he asked.

They both shook their heads no as Rex cowardly mumbled from under his absorbent two-ply shield of toilet paper, *"Not to my knowledge."*

Big Daddy relentlessly started fumbling through his pockets, turning them all inside out looking for the card. "I have it here somewhere! It's shaped like a magnifying glass," he said.

Big Daddy dug deep into his right shirt pocket and explained as he pulled out the card, "That evening after Big Mama and I discovered the cows missing, I went hog wild, searching high and low this entire ranch for 'em. All of a sudden, a warm gust of flowery-smellin' wind blew past my nose, and this card came floating right out of the sky."

Holding the crumpled business card, he snarled, "See, it's right here." He then read the card out loud,

"Moustachio Investigations,
Mysteries Are Our Specialty."

"Son," he grumbled, remembering Jake didn't solve the crime yet, "ya' need a new slogan!"

Mystified, Jake asked, "May I see that?"

"I reckon so," said Big Daddy.

Just as he was about to hand Jake the card, a warm gust of lilac-smelling air blew past them, picking up the card and blowing it far off into the wind. They followed its path as it disappeared into the grey haze of the further-eclipsed sky.

Rex popped his frizzy head out from under the toilet paper and wondered, "*Is it O.K. to come out, now?*"

"Yes," Jake nodded, disappointed at not having seen the card.

Rex jumped up, brushed himself off, and darted out of the grazing field to the un-toilet-papered ground.

Alexa noticed something dangling from Rex's tail as he scooted by. "The card—" she exclaimed, "it's stuck on Rex's tail!"

With a grin wider than the Grand Canyon, Jake rushed over to Rex and ripped the card from his furry butt. "*Ouch!*" he cried. "*Do you mind?*"

Jake quickly grabbed his magnifying glass from his back pocket and started examining every inch of the card. "This isn't the card," he announced with a puzzled look in his eye. "It's a ticket stub of some sort. Why, it's a bus ticket stub from Jacksboro to Tatterville, and it's from the night the cows were **kidnapped!**"

"Well—where the heck did that come from?" asked Big Daddy.

"It must have been buried in the ball," surmised Jake.

"Buried?" asked Alexa. "But we made the ball when we cleaned up the barn. I don't recall seeing that bus ticket."

"*I've never seen it before, either!*" exclaimed Rex, shaking his head.

Sandy, remembering she had found the ticket in the barn, jumped into Alexa's backpack and zipped herself in, hiding in shame.

"*All right, pig breath,*" bellowed Rex, "*spill it!*"

Sandy mumbled from beneath the pink nylon and purple leather of the Inspector Girl backpack, "I tried to tell you I fff—f—found the ticket, but no one would listen. You guys were so busy looking for clues and cleaning up the barn, I—I forgot. I—I must have wrapped it with the toilet paper into the ball. I'm sss—s—so sorry!"

"It's O.K., sweetie," Alexa said as she unzipped the backpack and scooped her up. "We really should be paying more attention to you. You're becoming quite the little detective."

Jake just stood there holding the ticket, staring at the moon as it continued to eclipse the sun. He remembered the story about Great-Great-Grandma Mary's father delivering mail along the Red River from Jacksboro. "I don't believe it!" he shouted. "We've been here all along."

"Been where?" asked Alexa.

"Here!" exclaimed Jake as he showed her the ticket. "Jacksboro and the Red River—it's all here!"

"*You mean this is where Great-Great-Grandma Mary's father delivered the mail?*" questioned Rex.

"Yep!" rattled Jake. "Lexy, do you still have that article on the solar eclipse?"

"I think so," she said, rummaging through her backpack. Alexa found the article she was saving for school and handed it to Jake.

He quickly read the article, pointed to the sky, and explained, "This type of eclipse hasn't happened for over a hundred years."

"That must explain why the sky suddenly became dark that night in Grandma's story," squealed Alexa. "The eclipse that is happening now is the same eclipse that was happening then."

"Right you are, Inspector Girl!" exclaimed Jake.

"That's all fine and dandy," interrupted Big Daddy, "but I still don't have my cows or the treasure."

"*Big Daddy's story from the auction is very similar to Grandma's,*" added Rex.

"Right again," noted Jake as he walked among the piles of toilet paper. "The stranger in Grandma's story offered Great-Great-Grandma Mary's father cattle that would lead him to a hidden treasure deep within the canyons. That canyon has to be somewhere around here."

"It's the west, son—" reminded Big Daddy. "We have lots of canyons in these parts."

"Oh," shouted Alexa, "I get it. One of the cows Chief Buffalo Hump sold you has a marking on it," Alexa said to Big Daddy.

"And that marking is definitely a hidden treasure map," declared Jake. "The map and the cattle the stranger offered Great-Great-Grandma Mary's father has to be that same map and cattle Big Daddy bought at the auction."

"*That's crazy!*" Rex snickered. "*That was over a hundred years ago.*"

"But he never read the map," explained Jake. "Don't you remember? The wind kicked up and blew his mail all over the place. He never had a chance to see the cattle or the stranger after he gathered up all his mail."

"So that means the treasure is still here somewhere?"

questioned Bob Billy Bob, scratching his head in confusion.

"Do you think the stranger in Grandma's story was Chief Buffalo Hump?" asked Alexa.

"*Now that's definitely crazy!*" laughed Rex. "*What do you suppose? He's a two hundred-year-old Indian?*"

"The greatest gift in life, my fine, furry, little friend, is your power to believe," declared Jake. "And I choose to believe this to be true!"

"Me, too!" exclaimed Alexa. "After all, mysteries are our specialty."

Jake paced back and forth re-examining the ticket stub, desperately trying to put all the clues together in his head in order to find the cows and wrap up this mystery. **Tatterville, Tatterville, he kept saying to himself.** "Tatterville!" he exclaimed. "That's where Daisy-Mae went to visit her mother."

"*Rufus didn't drive her there himself the night the cows were taken, did he?*" questioned Rex.

"No, he didn't!" Jake shouted in excitement. "He put her on a bus. This ticket proves it!"

"He lied to us," declared a disturbed Alexa.

"He did more than that," explained Jake. "He stole those cows, and we have the evidence to put him away!"

Big Daddy stomped all around, angrily throwing toilet paper into the eerie, darkening sky, "Let me at that scoundrel," he snarled. "Why—I'll tar and feather him!"

Jake looked up and gazed at the eclipsed sky. Mesmerized by the beauty of the moon's journey as it slowly covered the brilliance of the sun's glow, he remembered what Chief Buffalo Hump said to Big Daddy right before he disappeared.

"When the pale moon rises in front of the sun god, the path to a sacred Indian ground will be revealed on the hide of the chosen cow. Treasures will await you at the end of your journey."

"Ohhhhh, Nooooo!" he cried, in a panic.

Startled, Alexa asked, "What's wrong?"

"I'll explain on the way!" he shouted as he jumped up onto Bernardo's back. Jake signaled to Alexa, Sandy, and Rex to join him.

"Where are ya' going?" Big Daddy shouted in his deep burly voice.

"We're going back to the Giddy Goat Ranch to get your cows!" Jake explained, with a determined look in his eyes.

"What?" cried Rex in a huff. *"Are you out of your mind? Those henchmen are just waiting for us to go back up that hill. They'll wipe us out if they catch us! We'll never make it! We're doomed! Doomed, I tell ya'!"*

Big Daddy popped two oversized fingers into his mouth and blew a whistle that could be heard for miles. Galloping up the pasture came two of his finest, black Arabian stallions responding to his call.

As Big Daddy and Bob Billy Bob saddled up on the sturdy-looking horses, he bellowed, "Don't worry, little fella'. We'll ride shotgun to protect ya' from any dastardly sidewinders. Nothin's gonna stop me from getting my cows back."

"Did he say ride shotgun or bring a shotgun?" questioned Rex. *"Not that I condone firearms in any way, but in this case I'd make an exception."*

"Bernardo!" hollered out Jake. "The cows are in Miss Sally-Mae's pink barn. We have to get back to the Giddy Goat Ranch as fast as you can!"

Bob Billy Bob sat there on top of his horse with an unusual amount of sweat dripping from his forehead.

Noticing the sweat dripping from his brow, an angry look came across Big Daddy's face as he growled, "Boy, I know you've been messing around at that goat ranch. But if you've doubled-crossed me and had anything to do with my cows being kidnapped, taking a bath in horse manure will seem like a picnic compared to what I'm gonna do to ya'."

Bob Billy Bob shook in his saddle, not saying a word.

"Okey dokey, then!" exclaimed Big Daddy. "May the wind be at our backs and the bugs off our teeth!"

"*We're doomed!*" whimpered Rex, collapsing on Bernardo's back. "*Doomed!*"

CHAPTER FIFTEEN

I Knew It

The group galloped fast and furiously up the Red River once again towards the Giddy Goat Ranch.

Jake held firmly onto Bernardo's horns, guiding him, while Big Daddy's black stallions followed closely behind, ready to protect them at a moment's notice.

"*What's the rush?*" asked Rex. "*It's not like those stupid cows are going anywhere.*"

"I'm not worried about the cows," announced Jake. "It's the eclipse we have to worry about."

"What do you mean?" asked Alexa as she bounced all over Bernardo's back.

"Chief Buffalo Hump told Big Daddy at the auction 'when the pale moon rises in front of the sun god, the path to a sacred Indian ground will be revealed on the hide of the chosen cow. Treasures will await you at the end of your journey,'" explained Jake.

"*So?*" snipped Rex.

"He was describing a total solar eclipse, you knucklehead," Jake said.

"Oh, I get it," surmised Alexa. "The pale moon rising in front of the sun god is when the moon covers the rays of the sun."

"That's right," announced Jake. "When the moon covers the last bit of the sun, beams of light reflect off the moon's surface, creating an effect called 'Baily's beads.' "

Alexa grabbed the article from her backpack and quickly read it. "The beads shining around the moon look like a chain of bright glowing pearls," she explained.

"That's correct, Inspector Girl," added Jake. "During this very short part of the eclipse, the reflections of Baily's beads have been known to cause people to see things they normally could not see."

"*So, that must have been what Chief Buffalo Hump meant by the path to a sacred Indian ground will be revealed on the hide of the chosen cow,*" deducted Rex.

"Clever cat!" exclaimed Jake. "If we find the cow when the Baily's beads appear, we will be able to read the treasure map to the ancient Indian burial ground on the hide of that cow and, therefore, find the treasure."

"*And if we don't?*" asked Rex.

"The map and the treasure will be lost until the next complete solar eclipse," answered Jake.

"BBB—B—But that could be over another hundred years from now!" shouted Sandy, popping her head out of the corner of Alexa's backpack.

"That's why we have to hurry," yelled Jake. "We're running out of time. The moon has almost completely covered the sun. Once that happens, the Baily's beads will appear only lasting a few minutes."

"Faster, Bernardo, faster," they all yelled.

There was no sign of the dastardly henchmen as they galloped through the hazy landscape.

"Lexy, do you still have the booklet of five gift certificates Rupert gave us from The Library of Time?" Jake asked.

"Yep!" she exclaimed.

"Good," shouted Jake, "cause if we need a little extra help we can always stop time, but only if we have to!"

"What do you mean, stop time?" Rex alarmingly cried out.

"Each gift certificate Rupert gave us will stop time for one minute," explained Alexa.

"All we have to do is rip one certificate out of the booklet and throw it into the wind," added Jake.

"Wouldn't we have to be in really deep doo-doo to need them?" questioned Rex as his whiskers twitched in fear.

"Don't worry," Jake said with sheer confidence.

"What do you mean, don't worry?" muttered Rex. *"You've never stopped time before. How do you know we won't be zapped into dust and scattered across the universe or something? We're doomed. Doomed, I tell ya'!"*

"Rupert would never let anything happen to us," Alexa declared.

"Don't be such a scaredy cat!" added Jake, guiding Bernardo to the ranch.

They continued to gallop up the Red River at full speed, splashing water and kicking river rock with every twist and turn they made.

"Where are we headed, Inspector?" asked Big Daddy as they approached the broken gates of the Giddy Goat Ranch.

"To Sally-Mae's pink barn," he shouted. "And step on it—we don't have much time!"

Stampeding onto the ranch, they ran right past the Nanny Goat sisters still hanging out at the front door. The bells dangling from their necks rang out loud from the force of the wind as they all blew past.

"Well, hello to you from me!" greeted Fannie.

"And a hello from me to you, too!" Annie added.

The group was in such a hurry they had no time to chit-chat with the sisters.

"How utterly and completely rude!" observed Fannie.

"I would most definitely have to agree with you, dear sister!" snorted Annie.

Sandy looked back and saw them out of the corner of the backpack and squeaked, "Hi, mmm—m—my name's Sandy. What's yours?"

Exasperated, the two old goats looked at each other.

"Oh, dear," sighed Fannie, "that poor, poor guinea pig has completely lost her mind."

"Completely, dear sister," murmured Annie, "completely!"

While bouncing all around the Inspector Girl backpack, Sandy murmured to Alexa, "They seem like very nice goats. We should go back later and introduce ourselves."

As Alexa protectively shoved Sandy to the bottom of the backpack and zipped her up, she scolded, "You've met them three times now, sweetie. You really do need to start writing these things down!"

"I'm a guinea pig," she mumbled from inside the backpack. I don't know how to www—w—write."

"Well, we'll just have to work on that," declared Alexa.

Bernardo and the two black stallions thundered toward the pink barn with determination. Hearing and seeing all the commotion, Rufus McGraw, his daughter, Sally-Mae, and her precious pig, Magnolia, came running to the scene.

"What are y'all doing here?" questioned Rufus in a huff, blocking the white doors to the barn. "Big Daddy, now you get off my land or I'll—"

"Or you'll what, you backstabbin' scoundrel?" roared

back Big Daddy.

"Why—I'll just call the sheriff!" threatened Sally-Mae, adjusting her crooked tiara on her perfectly combed, raven-colored head.

"That's right—" scoffed Rufus. "We'll call the sheriff."

"Well, you go right ahead and do that!" dared Jake as he approached the barn doors, glaring at him. "We'll invite him right into your barn so he can look for those cows you— ***kidnapped!***"

"I told you I was driving my wife to Tatterville that night," declared Rufus. "I couldn't possibly have taken those cows!"

Jake reached into his pocket, pulled out the bus ticket stub, waved it into Rufus's face and announced, "Then how do you explain— ***this!***"

Rufus glanced at the stub and denied ever seeing it before.

"I know you did it!" Jake cried, pushing him aside as he reached for the door.

"Let me at 'im," grunted Big Daddy. "I'll twist him right up into a pretzel."

"Not yet!" exclaimed Jake to Big Daddy.

Panicking, Bob Billy Bob cut off Jake by blocking the door. "Ya' can't go in there, Inspector," he yelled. "I won't let ya'!"

"I knew he did it!" yelled Alexa with a smile on her face. "Inspector Girl can smell a culprit a mile away. Bob Billy Bob must have hid out behind the barn and waited for Little Big Daddy's bed time so no one would be around. He was wearing his yellow-straw hat and eating popcorn during the kidnapping. That's why there was popcorn at the cow barn and yellow straw behind this one where he hid the cows." She then scurried over to the doors and pushed Bob Billy Bob right out of the way.

"Let me at him," snarled Big Daddy. "I'll cover him in honey and hang him near a beehive!"

"Not just yet!" ordered Jake, again, to Big Daddy.

Jake gave Alexa an annoyed look and snapped, "That's not right! What about the goat bell and the other clues?"

Just as Alexa was about to open the barn doors, Sally-Mae threw herself across them, pushed Alexa out of the way, and shouted with an evil glimmer in her crystal-clear, blue eyes, "Don't even think about it, missy!"

"*Ahhh-ha, I knew it!*" uttered Rex. "*She did it! She waited for everyone to be asleep and for her father to drive her mother to Tatterville. And while that ridiculous-looking pig was munching on popcorn, they grabbed the cows and rushed them over here. When they were hustling the cows out of Big Daddy's barn, the pig dropped the tiara she was wearing. Step aside, Critter Detective is going into that barn to solve the case!*"

"Let me at that pig!" shouted Big Daddy. "Why, I'll turn her into bacon bits."

"Not quite yet!" soothed Jake, trying to calm Big Daddy's boiling-mad temper.

Jake picked up Rex, looked him square in the eye and shouted, crinkling his nose, "Look at my face, you over-grown hair ball. We don't have much time left and that makes absolutely no sense. I am not wrong. Rufus stole those cows, and I'm going to tell you all how—*RIGHT HERE—AND RIGHT NOW!*

"At the cattle auction, Rufus heard Big Daddy and Chief

Buffalo Hump negotiating over the sale of those cows. More cows for Big Daddy meant more cow milk, making Big Daddy even bigger than before. You, Rufus, must have been in a jealous rage, and that's when you got the idea to kidnap his cows," explained Jake, pointing at Rufus.

"*But Rufus probably got distracted when Sally-Mae came in whining about needing money to open up her pig grooming parlor*," Rex announced as he stroked his whiskers.

"I don't whine, you annoying feline!" snapped Sally-Mae. "It's not ladylike."

"You never heard Chief Buffalo Hump explaining to Big Daddy about the treasure map on the hide of one of the cows, did you, Rufus?" questioned Jake.

They all gasped, "***Treasure!***" in utter surprise. "What treasure?"

"He didn't!" proclaimed Alexa. "Because if he, or any one of you had heard, you would be looking for the map right now; after all, the eclipse is almost complete."

"You needed a solid alibi, didn't you, Mr. McGraw?" asked Jake. "When your mother-in-law became sick, you had it! You let everyone think you drove your wife to her mother's in Tatterville. Knowing no one would ever know otherwise, you bought Daisy-Mae a bus ticket and sent her on her way alone. My guess is, she was wearing her favorite tiara at the time. You know—the one with the black metallic pearl in the center that's missing from your trophy case. But before she left, she probably didn't want to travel with such a cherished possession, so she handed you her prized tiara for safekeeping. You must have put it in one of your pockets along with her torn bus ticket stub."

Alexa rummaged through her backpack with Sandy's help and pulled out the tiara with the metallic black pearl in the center. "This is it!" she announced as she held it up high.

Sally-Mae let out a high-pitched shriek, "That's my mother's favorite tiara." She snatched it right out of Alexa's hand. "Where did you get this?" she asked.

"*We found it in Big Daddy's cow barn,*" explained Rex.

"Now how did that ever get there?" Sally-Mae asked.

"My guess is your father must have dropped that tiara and this bus ticket in Big Daddy's barn when he was rustling the cows," Jake said as he waved the stub.

Sally-Mae stomped right over to her father waving the tiara madly under his nose. "Rufus McGraw, is this what you lost of Mama's? You're going to be in so much trouble when she gets back home," she warned.

"But Jake, how did he get all those cows off Big Daddy's ranch over to this pink barn?" Alexa asked.

"I think he used that nasty goat that butt-kicked Rex to scare the cows off Big Daddy's ranch. You know, the one with the black patch on his right eye and the sharp ivory horns," replied Jake. "He's a stubborn animal. My guess is, he wouldn't cooperate with you, Rufus, so you lured him over to Big Daddy's with the popcorn."

"*That's why I found the left over popcorn kernels on the floor at the barn,*" piped up Rex.

"That's right, my pesky pet," cheered Jake. "All the goats at the Giddy Goat Ranch have bells around their necks. That's how you can tell one from another. But that goat is missing his bell."

"*So, the bell I cut my paw on belongs to that nasty goat*

that kicked me clear across the sky?" Rex groaned out as he licked his wounded paw.

Jake was pacing back and forth in front of Rufus and the white barn doors. "My guess is that while you were struggling to move so many cows at one time, the bell with the magnolia flower fell right off the neck of that nasty, old goat and landed out by Big Daddy's grazing field fence."

"But what about the yellow-hay hat, Jake?" Alexa asked, thoughtfully.

"I'll bet Rufus saw Bob Billy Bob forgetting his hat at the auction," Jake surmised.

"I get it!" exclaimed Alexa. "Rufus grabbed the hat and wore it the night of the kidnapping."

"Right you are, my clever sister," shouted Jake. "If anyone saw him from a distance, they would think it was Bob Billy Bob checking on the cows. No one would be suspicious of him doing his job. He's supposed to be there!"

"That made for a perfect disguise," agreed Rex.

"The hole in the hat must have happened when Rufus was shoving the cows into this pink barn," explained Jake. "My guess is, one of the horns from the black-eyed goat must have pierced the hat, tearing the hole in the back."

"Then that would explain the funny-looking, yellow-hay shavings you found behind the barn," replied Rex.

"It's elementary, my good pussy cat!" nodded Jake, "Elementary! Some of the yellow hay we found must have fallen off the cows, and the rest of the yellow hay that got oxidized, turning slightly brown on the edges, came from the hole made in Bob Billy Bob's hat!"

CHAPTER SIXTEEN

Cownapper

"But if Rufus McGraw kidnapped the cows," questioned Alexa, "why do Bob Billy Bob and Sally-Mae keep blocking the barn doors?"

"MMM—M—Maybe they were all in on it," guessed Sandy as she inquisitively popped her head out of the backpack.

Jake paced back and forth in front of his collection of suspects while they glared back with guilt and secrecy. "No, those two," he stated as he pointed to Sally-Mae and Bob Billy Bob, "are guilty of something, but I don't think they had anything to do with the missing cows."

Jake slowly moved closer and closer to the white barn doors, as Rufus, Bob Billy Bob, Sally-Mae, and Magnolia moved even closer in—trying to block his entry.

Big Daddy was madder than a squirrel without nuts. "Let me at them!" he shouted. "They're nothin' but a bunch of yellow-bellied snakes. Why, I'm gonna feed them to a hungry mountain lion—as soon as I find one!"

Tightly pressed up against the barn doors, the three suspicious looking characters and Magnolia gasped in terror.

Looking at the eclipse that was almost finished, Jake announced, "The mountain lion might be a good idea, but unless you have one handy, we don't have enough time."

Jake signaled Bernardo. "Can you break down those doors?" he asked.

Bernardo wiped the last drop of tears from his eyes and nodded yes as his glistening copper nose ring wagged in the musty air.

Sally-Mae cried out loud, "You wouldn't!"

"*Desperate times call for desperate measures!*" Rex exclaimed with a big grin.

"Bernardo," ordered Jake, pointing to the pink barn, "The cows are in **THERE!**"

Bernardo got a determined look across his face; steam came pouring out of his nostrils. He revved himself up like the engine of a drag racing car about to zip across the starting line and took off in a fury, heading straight for Rufus, Sally-Mae, Bob Billy Bob, and Magnolia. He rammed through the barn doors, bursting them wide open while everyone jumped out of his way, screaming for their lives.

Bernardo stampeded into the barn, crashing into a long row of pink chairs that had large, silver, helmet-like hair dryers attached to their backs. Dazed, he stood up with a hair dryer helmet stuck on his poor, confused head.

They all went running frantically into the barn to see what all the commotion was about.

"Now look what you've done," scolded Sally-Mae with a nasty glare in her eyes. "My hair dryers are ruined!"

"Hair dryers!" frowned Jake. He quickly grabbed his magnifying glass and searched every corner of the barn baffled and confused.

"*Where are the cows?*" screeched Rex, tagging behind Jake in the hunt.

Rufus was more shocked than anyone at the

transformation of the barn and the lack of any cows. His old, messy goat barn had been converted into the most beautiful pig beauty parlor they had ever seen. Inside, it was the size of a football field. The walls were draped in pink and purple satin curtains, while the floor was covered in a soft white sheepskin rug. There were lotions and creams that smelled like fruits and flowers with curlers and bows bursting out of boxes, which were stacked up high to the newly painted, pink, wood rafters of the ceiling. Lipstick tubes and numerous other make-up baskets crammed every shelf as far as the eye could see.

"Is it me," Jake asked Rex, "or is this barn bigger on the inside than it looks on the outside?"

"Now, let me get this straight!" Rex answered. *"You're talking to your pet cat, searching for a pink, white or brown kidnapped cow that has a treasure map on its hide that you can only see during a complete solar eclipse. And the last time this happened was when your great-great-grandmother's father was delivering mail in these parts. We're being chased by an evil Baron who wants to steal your grandfather's mystical magnifying glass so he can stop you from solving all the mysteries of the universe, and you think it's strange that the inside of this tiny barn is the size of a football field?"*

"Why, yes—I do!" snapped Jake as he continued his investigation.

"Oh, brother!" sighed Rex.

"Sally-Mae," Rufus yelled in a fit of anger. "What have ya' done to my barn?"

"Isn't it fabulous!" she squealed, too excited to contain herself. "We did all this in the past two days."

Alexa and Sandy nodded their heads in agreement on the beauty of the barn as they started fiddling with a box of striped, silk, pink bows.

"Pink is my signature color," boasted Alexa. "I love all things pink: pink ribbons, pink clothes, pink nails, and especially strawberry milk from pink cows!"

"Me ttt—t—too!" Sandy said dreamily.

"You know," added Alexa, "my friend, Grace—her favorite color is brown. I just don't get that color."

"How sad," sighed Sally-Mae with a perplexed look. "Pink is just so much more alive and vibrant than brown, really!"

"Where are my pink cows?" Big Daddy grimaced, stomping all around the barn, searching every box and crate he could find.

"Who's we?" Rufus demanded of Sally-Mae.

"Why Maggie and I," Sally-Mae declared. "And Bob Billy Bob, of course."

"Bob Billy Bob!" they all spouted.

"Bob Billy Bob and I are in love," she explained.

"We're getting married," he said. "I gave Sally-Mae half the money she needed to start up her pig beauty parlor."

"And after I sell all my pig calendars featuring my precious Maggie," assured Sally-Mae, "we'll have enough money to finish it all up!"

Sally-Mae darted over to a large billboard leaning up against the corner wall and pulled off the sheet covering it. The sign read, "***Sally-Mae's Pig Emporium: No Pig Is Too Ugly To Be Beautiful!***"

"*She really is crazy!*" Rex snapped bluntly.

Rufus was furious that his daughter set up her new

business behind his back. He pounced right over to her and demanded to know what she had done with all those cows.

"What cows?" she protested. "The barn was empty when we started to set this all up."

She looked at her father with a disappointed frown and hollered, "Rufus McGraw, I'm ashamed of you. You **did** take those cows! Didn't you?"

She grabbed a pig tail curling iron, waved it wildly in the air like a sword, and ranted, "Mama's going to be so mad when she gets back from Tatterville. If you're in prison, who's going to give me away at my wedding?"

Rufus's guilty face was beet red. "I did it for you, sugar plum, so I could make more money with my goat milk and goat buttered popcorn. I wanted you and your mother to be proud of me. I was going to build ya' your very own pig beauty parlor as a surprise."

"Don't you blame this on me, you cownapper!" she accused in a piercing tone. "You kidnapped those cows for yourself. You just couldn't stand Big Daddy's being bigger than you. You've wanted to ruin him for years. You took those cows to help yourself, not me!"

"But, sugar plum!" denied Rufus.

"Just look at your granddaughter's sad, disappointing snout," she uttered, staring sadly at Magnolia. "And right before my wedding!"

"*Did she just call that stupid pig in that ridiculous tiara his granddaughter?*" Rex snickered.

Nodding her head in an unbelievable yes, Alexa answered, "I believe she did."

Big Daddy stomped over to Rufus with anger boiling from ear to ear. The spurs on his boots clanked against the floor, echoing throughout the barn. He grabbed Rufus by the shoulders and pulled him up to look him square in the eyes. Rufus cowardly shook in his boots, frightened at what was to come. Everyone gasped in fear. "Rufus," he snarled, "where are my darn cows?"

Dangling three feet off the ground, Rufus uttered, "I haven't got the foggiest idea! I left them here three days ago! The Inspector was right—the goat and I rustled them all over here that night, and it took forever. That large, pink cow with the brown patch on her butt, Darlene, kept biting me on the head. That's how the hole got into Bob Billy Bob's hat. She put up quite a fight."

Bernardo let out a pathetic scream, crashing to the floor, and cried his eyes out over the loss of his beloved Darlene. Sally-Mae's sheepskin rug was getting drenched in bull tears.

"Stop that, you stupid bull!" she scolded, tugging him off the rug by his nose ring. "You're ruining my new rug."

Big Daddy, still firmly holding Rufus in mid-air, bellowed, "Darlene is Bernardo's favorite cow, you scoundrel!"

"Sally-Mae," Rufus cried out, looking to her for help.

"Oh, no!" she argued. "You got yourself into this mess and you're going to get yourself out of it—on your own!"

The loud, never-ending bickering between everyone over the missing cows made Jake more determined than ever to solve this mystery. With his magnifying glass in hand, and Rex traipsing close behind, Jake combed the enormous interior of the tiny pink barn searching to find any clues that would lead him to the missing cows.

"Here cowy, cowy," sung Rex. *"Where, oh where, have the big cows gone? Oh where, oh where have they gone? Here cowy, cowy."*

Suddenly, Jake heard the most wickedly evil laugh echoing from the rafters. "Shush!" he whispered to Rex as he covered his hand over his whiskered singing mouth.

"I can't breathe," Rex mumbled from underneath. *"You're smothering me!"*

Jake heard the laugh again. It was even louder this time. He slowly removed his hand from over Rex's mouth, signaling him not to speak. "I think there's someone here," he whispered into his furry pal's ear.

"Where?" Rex questioned, in an almost silent tone. *"I don't hear anything. And you know cats can hear everything!"*

Jake's big green eyes flew wide open as the laughter got closer, and louder, and closer, and even louder.

"Hello, Inspector," said the creepy voice.

Jake was paralyzed with fear as he frantically scanned the barn for the whereabouts of the devilish voice.

"Don't bother looking for me, dear boy. This is a trick I learned many years ago. You see—I'm not really here! I'm in your mind, my young Moustachio!"

As the voice let out another malicious laugh, Jake's heart began to beat faster and faster. His face turned as white as a ghost. The nervous sweat dripping from the palm of his hand made the magnifying glass slippery to the touch.

"I've waited a long time to meet the next Inspector Moustachio—a very, very long, long

time. **Allow me to introduce myself, as if you didn't already know.**" The voice chuckled scornfully. "**I am—** *Baron Von Snodgrass!*"

Shocked, Jake lost his grip on the magnifying glass. It slipped right out of his hand and clunked Rex forcefully on the head.

"*Ouch!*" Rex cried as he swatted Jake with his left paw and rubbed his fuzzy, bruised noggin with the other. "*Watch that thing, would ya'!*"

Jake trembled as he bent down and picked up the magnifying glass. A luminous, blue glow of light emanated from it, almost blinding him as he held it in his hand.

"**Can you feel the power, young Moustachio?**" echoed Snodgrass in Jake's head. "**The closer the magnifying glasses are to each other, my young friend, the more you will be able to hear and feel my presence. And I'm a lot closer than you realize. I have your precious cows and the eclipse draws soon to an end! You might want to hurry, dear boy, the clock is ticking for you to be able to read the treasure map. *TICK-TOCK, TICK-TOCK—***

"**You know, I grow weary of *THESE COWS!* Why, I think I will destroy them, *ONE BY ONE!* Especially the big pink one with the brown patch on her butt, she annoys me most—*OF ALL!***

"**No more cow milk for your breakfast tables, dear boy! No more ice cream or Clunky Chunky Chocolate Bars!**" he cried out in an endless, horrific laugh.

"**It will all be gone *FOREVER! UNLESS*—you can stop me! The cows and the map are at Comanche**

Canyon, young Moustachio! We're waiting—*FOR YOU!*"

In a panic, Jake started running towards the barn doors.

"*Where are you going?*" shouted Rex as he scurried behind.

"The cows are at Comanche Canyon," explained Jake, racing past the group. "He's going to destroy them if we don't hurry!"

"Who, Jake?" cried out Alexa, zipping up Sandy safely into the backpack, and dashing close behind him.

"Snodgrass!" he exclaimed shakily. "That's who!"

Everyone gasped in disbelief and ran frantically after Jake, following him outside.

"Who's this Snodgrass fella'? And why does he have my cows?" bellowed Big Daddy, stroking the ruff stubble of his cleft chin.

"Do you remember that odd looking stranger at the auction?" Jake asked. "You know, the one slithering around, acting suspiciously?"

"Yeah," recalled Big Daddy. "He had on the funniest coat. It was a long, yellow, linen duster draped all over him like a magician's cape."

"Why, I remember him!" exclaimed Sally-Mae. "I never forget a face, especially one of the male persuasion. He had an odd, flat, brimmed hat slightly covering a jagged scar running through his tiny, black moustache on the right side of his face. Why, I do recall it almost looked like the letter *M*."

"The Baron stole the cows after Rufus kidnapped them. That's why the barn was empty when Sally-Mae and Bob

Billy Bob started setting up the pig parlor," Jake explained.

"*So the kidnapped cows got kidnapped from the first kidnapper by a second kidnapper!*" exclaimed Rex, dizzy from his explanation.

"So I'm off the hook?" Rufus hopefully asked.

Big Daddy got right down ever-so-closely into Rufus's now trembling face. He could smell the barbeque sauce on Big Daddy's breath from the spareribs he ate earlier. "I don't think so, you cownapping scallywag!" Big Daddy proclaimed. "You're going up the river!"

"But what would that badly dressed gentleman want with those silly, old cows anyway?" questioned Sally-Mae.

"He doesn't want the cows," explained Jake. "He wants the magnifying glass, and he's using the cows to lure us right to him!"

"*It's a trap!*" screeched Rex as he clawed his way into the Inspector Girl backpack to hide. "*We're doomed, I tell ya'! Doomed as doomed can be!*"

Rex jumped in, zipped himself up and hid at the bottom of the backpack with Sandy. Realizing there wasn't enough room for the two animals, he unzipped it and booted Sandy out head first. Alexa leaped forward and caught Sandy just as she went flying into the hazy, grey, sun-eclipsed sky.

"Rex," she scolded as she unzipped her backpack, "you get out of there! I can't carry both of you, and Sandy is way too small to keep up with us on her own."

Rex reluctantly crawled out and slithered shamelessly away. Alexa placed Sandy safely back where she belonged.

"What are we going to do, Jake?" she asked.

As Jake looked up at the solar eclipse, he could see the start of the beams of light coming from the moon's surface creating the Baily's beads effect. "We're almost out of time," he warned. "Once the Baily's beads completely shine around the moon, that treasure map will appear on the hide of one of those cows for only a minute or so!"

"That's it?" exclaimed Big Daddy, stomping all around in a sudden, overwhelming fright. "We only have a minute or two?"

"That's it!" shouted Jake with a determined look in his eyes. "How do we get to Comanche Canyon?"

Pointing off to the West, Bob Billy Bob yelled, "It's beyond that ridge, that-a-way!"

"It's twenty minutes by horse, Inspector," announced Big Daddy, his brows creased with worry.

Alexa's big blue eyes widened as she realized, "We're not going to make it!"

Jake stood there courageously holding his grandpa's magnifying glass, determined to solve this case and save the cows. He remembered what Delbert had told him, ***"Your magnifying glass and you are one. The power within you controls the power within the magnifying glass. Master your mind and thoughts and you will be able to learn how to control the magnifying glass."***

"This isn't over yet—Inspector Girl!" Jake assured. With all the strength in his body, he threw the magnifying glass into the sky and yelled out loud—
"COMANCHE CANYON!"

An enormous bolt of lightning shot out of the magnifying glass as it soared through the air. Hitting the ground, a pool of blinding light radiated from it as it grew larger and larger. A vortex of wind spun from the glass blowing everything and everyone in its path.

"Let's go!" shouted Jake to Alexa and Rex, above the ferocious wind.

Everyone else stood in speechless awe at the powers of the magnifying glass and the spectacular events unfolding before their eyes.

"*Are you crazy?*" whined Rex. "*Snodgrass will obliterate us into nothing the moment we fall out of that magnifying glass.*"

"It's a chance we'll have to take," declared Jake.

Alexa shivered in fear as Jake tightly held her hand. He reassured her that he would let nothing happen to her or Sandy. Rex jumped into the safety of Jake's arm, his tail twice its normal size. Jake turned back to Big Daddy and yelled through the vortex of wind, "I'll get your cows back and the treasure. ***I promise!***"

On three, Jake, Alexa, Sandy, and Rex jumped into the tumultuous storm of the magnifying glass.

The rest of them just stood there in shock. "Well, what are y'all waiting for?" bellowed Big Daddy. "Isn't anyone going to jump in and help 'em?"

Sally-Mae winked her long, black eyelash over her sparkling, blue, right eye at Bob Billy Bob and declared, "Well—the Inspector did say treasure, now didn't he?" She scooped up Magnolia, grabbed his hand, and they jumped into the magnifying glass in hope of finding the treasure before anyone else did.

"Come on, Bernardo, we're going, too!" commanded Big Daddy.

As Rufus McGraw started to slither away, Big Daddy grabbed him from behind. "Where do you think you're going, you cowardly chicken?" He then plucked Rufus right up and threw him into the magnifying glass. Rufus's fearful cries echoed throughout the whirlpool of wind.

Big Daddy, in the biggest of ways, jumped on top of Bernardo, riding him straight into the vortex, and made a gigantic leap into the magnifying glass, bellowing, "May the wind be at our backs and the bugs off our teeth!"

CHAPTER SEVENTEEN

Comanche Canyon

As the children glided down the tornado-like funnel of wind, they were unaware of their uninvited guests sliding in hot pursuit right behind them. Faster and faster they all slid—twisting and turning with every bend as sparkles of color flew past their amazed eyes.

The children, with Rex and Sandy held tightly in their arms, came exploding out of the magnifying glass first, rolling like a bunch of loose tumbleweeds over the dry, dusty, amber-colored terrain. They marveled at the awesome sight of the magnificent canyon that had been carved through the rocks of the Jacksboro Plateau over years and years of forgotten time.

"Did we make it?" shrugged Alexa as she dusted herself off.

They quickly scanned the canyon for any signs of Snodgrass, but there was no sign of the evil Baron yet. But what they did find were rows of white, brown, and, yes, pink cows spread across the canyon for miles.

"I KNEW IT!" confirmed Alexa in a sassy tone. "Look before you, my dear brother. There they are—white, brown, and the pinkest of cows. *I WAS RIGHT!* Strawberry milk does come from pink cows, chocolate milk comes from brown cows, and white milk comes from white cows."

"Just because you see pink cows doesn't necessarily

mean they make pink milk!" Jake grunted in protest.

"What do I have to do, milk one for you?" she challenged.

"*Come on, throw her a bone, Inspector,*" suggested Rex.

Jake, never happy to be proven wrong, finally agreed. Chocolate milk must come from brown cows, white milk must come from white cows, and, therefore, by default, strawberry milk must come from the pinkest of pink cows.

"Hey," asked Sandy as she popped her head out from the Inspector Girl backpack, "why is the mmm—m—magnifying glass not shrinking?"

The vortex of wind was still being propelled from inside the glass. The children ran for cover behind a row of tall green prickly cactus bushes in fear for their young lives.

"*We're doomed!*" cried Rex. "*It's the evil Baron coming to wipe us out!*"

Suddenly, the magnifying glass shot out a bolt of light as Sally-Mae, Bob Billy Bob, and Magnolia came flying through. They fell face first into a big, old, banana yucca plant. "Now, just look at the mess in my hair!" exclaimed Sally-Mae as she untangled her tiara from the white, flowering, pointy plant. "And just look at Magnolia. **Yuck!** She's covered from snout to squiggly pig tail in yucca!"

The magnifying glass, still spewing a forceful wind, violently erupted again. Rufus McGraw shot out, followed by Bernardo carrying Big Daddy who screamed out, "Yahoo!" while leaping over everyone's head. Landing on the red rocky ground right in front of the cactus bushes the children were hiding behind, he shouted for joy, "**My cows! Inspector, ya' found my cows!**"

Big Daddy looked into the distance searching for the love of Bernardo's life, his special cow, Darlene. There she was, mooing, smack in the middle of the herd at the bottom of the canyon. Darlene was uncomfortably squashed between two big, old, brown and white cows. Bernardo's eyes lit up like the sun as he thoughtlessly dumped Big Daddy right on his butt and raced like the dickens to his favorite pink cow with the brown spot on her hide.

"Ahhh—true love!" sighed Alexa as she picked a yucca flower and sniffed its fragrant odor before placing it in her hair.

The vortex of wind collapsed into the magnifying glass as it shrank back to its normal size: a small, reddish dust ball puffed into the air as it hit the ground.

"*Yuck!*" Rex frowned as he scurried over to retrieve the magnifying glass. "*All this talk of lovey-dovey stuff is making me sick.*" He darted back over to the children and handed Jake the magnifying glass, who quickly scoped out the canyon for any signs of Snodgrass or his henchmen.

The solar eclipse was now complete. The beams of light bouncing off the moon's surface needed to read the treasure map were upon them.

"We need to split up," ordered Jake in a panic. "We only have a few minutes to find the right cow and read that treasure map before the Baily's beads disappear."

Big Daddy's black cowboy boots left gigantic imprints in the loose, sandy gravel as he stomped off in a hurry to search for his map.

Sally-Mae, Bob Billy Bob, Rufus, and Magnolia quietly sneaked off unnoticed by the children to search for the right cow on their own, hoping to find the map and the treasure for themselves.

"Lexy, do you still have that tracing paper you were using to copy the letter Great-Great-Grandma Mary wrote to Great-Great-Aunt Fay about her barbeque sauce recipe?" Jake hastily called out.

"I would never leave home without it!" Alexa cheered as she searched her backpack. She whipped out her tracing paper and her favorite long-stem, pink pencil with the pink, feathered ball at the end of the eraser. "But technically, it was only half a letter because the other half of the letter got lost. That's why Grandma can't make the barbeque sauce right because the missing ingredients are written on the other missing part of the letter."

A frustrated look flew across Jake's face. "As charming as that story sounds, my dear sister, we're running out of *TIME!*"

"You don't have to get snippy," she retorted.

"O.K.," explained Jake as he noticed everyone else searching for the map, "Here's what we're gonna do. Lexy and Sandy are going to search the canyon for the right cow. When you find the cow, trace the map from its hide onto your tracing paper, and whatever you do, don't let any of those nuts over there get a look at that map. Rex and I will search for Snodgrass."

"*Wait just a darn minute,*" complained Rex. "*Why does pig breath get the safe job? I want to go find the map. Let her go search for that evil Baron.*"

"Listen, you annoying fur ball, you're coming with me, and that's the way it's going to be," commanded Jake in a no-nonsense tone.

"*All right, you're the boss. You don't have to get snippy,*" Rex shrugged.

"I'm not being snippy!" he snipped. "Why does everyone

think I'm being snippy?"

Alexa and Sandy raced off in search of the cow with the map on its hide. Jake reminded them to keep the gift certificates from The Library of Time handy in case they got into trouble and needed to stop time.

The canyon was in utter chaos with the moos of the endless rows of cows echoing into the eerie, sun-eclipsed sky. Sally-Mae and Magnolia were systematically skipping from cow to cow, examining every inch of them for the map. Rufus, hesitantly, crawled on his back under the cows searching their bellies for any signs of strange markings. Bob Billy Bob haphazardly kept tipping over sleeping rows of cows hoping to speed up his search. And Big Daddy, led by Bernardo and Darlene, searched among their friends. Everyone selfishly wanted to find the map and the treasure that awaited the best scavenger hunter.

Suddenly, a crack of thunder crashed from above as a second magnifying glass appeared in the sky. It had the same golden frame and cherry wood handle as Jake's but was tarnished from years gone by. An evil laughter emanated from the smoky wind that steamed through the center of the glass.

Jake, trembling in fear, yelled out through the forceful blast of the wind, "No matter what happens, Inspector Girl, don't stop until you get that map. Promise me—"

Her clear blue eyes teared up, terrified for her brother, but she promised she wouldn't let him down.

Rex's tail stood straight up, shaking in the wind, his golden eyes wide open in horror. "We're doomed aren't we?" he winced.

"*YEAH—*" Jake agreed shakily, his heart beating faster and faster. "Are you with me?"

"*Where else would I be!*" assured Rex as he lovingly nuzzled Jake's leg. "*BRING IT ON!*"

CHAPTER EIGHTEEN

The Battle With The Baron

Slithering out from the smoky shadows of the magnifying glass was Baron Von Snodgrass. He looked just as Jake had imagined. His long, yellow, linen coat waved in the stormy air as it draped from his shoulders like the wings of a bat. His odd, flat-brimmed, black hat sat on his head, slightly covering the corner of his evil, dark, deep-set eyes. A familiar, blue handkerchief wrapped tightly around his face, hiding the jagged scar that ran through his tiny, black moustache. Tucked into his high, shiny, left boot for safe keeping was a small, weathered, brown, leather-bound book.

His seemingly endless wicked laughter pierced the endless moos of the cows. "*Omecay otay emay!*" he commanded to his magnifying glass as he extended his long, right arm and unraveled his boney fingers. The magnifying glass let out a burst of light, shrunk back to its original size, and flew directly into the palm of his hand.

"*WOW!*" uttered Rex. "*Can you do that?*"

"I don't think so!" Jake exclaimed with a puzzled look.

"Well! Well! Well!" laughed Snodgrass. "If it isn't Buck Moustachio's grandson in the flesh! I hope you haven't become too attached to that magnifying glass, young Moustachio, because I'm about to take it from you!"

Snarling, Snodgrass swirled his magnifying glass high

into the sky and yelled, "*Iway illway astblay ouyay intoway ethay eavenshay!*" Suddenly, a fiery bolt of lightning shot out of his magnifying glass towards Jake and Rex. They dove for cover behind a gigantic boulder as the bolt of lighting whizzed past them, exploding as it hit the ground.

"Well, I know I definitely don't know how to do that!" shrieked Jake in a panic as he covered their heads from the falling debris.

"*We're doomed!*" cried Rex.

"**JAKE!**" screamed out Alexa.

"I'm all right," he shouted. "Keep looking for that cow!"

Alexa hurried through the field of endless, white, brown, and, yes, pink cows with Sandy bouncing behind in her Inspector Girl backpack. "Do you see anything that looks like a map, sweetie?" she asked.

"NNN—N—Nothing!" answered Sandy.

They looked high and low on each and every cow for the treasure map but had no luck. It was one gigantic scavenger hunt with Sally-Mae, Bob Billy Bob, Rufus, Magnolia, Bernardo, Darlene, and Big Daddy all feverishly combing the canyon in different directions in hot pursuit to find the special cow first.

"No, not that one," mumbled Alexa.

"How aaa—a—about that one?" asked Sandy.

"No, no, not that one, either," she answered.

"What about that hot pink one with the lll—l—long eyelashes over her droopy eyes?" pondered Sandy.

Alexa ran to take a look. Her eyes lit up in excitement as she ran around the cow and saw to her complete surprise—

the map. It was painted on the right side of the hot-pink cow's hide with multicolored paints. Careful not to be noticed by the other treasure hunters, Alexa and Sandy very quietly, but quickly, pulled out the tracing paper and Alexa's long-stem, pink pencil with the pink, feathered ball at the end of the eraser. They got right to work tracing all the curves, trails, and landmarks from the cow onto the paper. The extremely ticklish, hot-pink cow started giggling and squirming with every line Alexa traced.

Sandy looked out into the canyon and saw the others getting closer. "Hurry, Alexa, hhh—h—hurry!" cried Sandy frantically.

"How are you doing, Lexy?" Jake's voice echoed throughout the canyon.

"I'm getting there!" she yelled in frustration. "If only this cow would stay still. I don't want to miss any part of this map."

Jake and Rex brushed the dirt and loose rocks off themselves as they crawled out from behind the boulder.

"Are you ready to give up, young Moustachio?" snickered Snodgrass.

"Not on your life," shouted out Jake.

"*Are you sure?*" whined Rex, clinging to Jake's leg. "*You might want to re-think that!*"

"**SO, THE BATTLE BEGINS!**" hissed Snodgrass.

"What have you done with Mrs. Smythe?" shouted Jake over the blustery wind.

"Oh, she's floating around somewhere getting ready to bake something poisonous, I suppose. I plucked her right out of that prison. It wasn't very difficult, my young Moustachio. That stupid giraffe didn't know what hit him! Be careful who you trust, dear boy. Delbert hides things from you!" The Baron laughed as he raised his magnifying glass into the wind, and with a treacherous look in his eyes, he yelled, **"Egonebay!"**

Hysterical, Rex screamed out, "*What did he say? What did he say?*"

Baron Von Snodgrass's magnifying glass started to rumble in his hand as it let out an enormous bolt of hot, sizzling lightning.

"Jump!" cried Jake to Rex. "Jump!"

They barely escaped with their lives as the bolt flew passed their heads. Jake and Rex tumbled over a cliff, falling below on top of a startled Sally-Mae and Magnolia, who were still searching for the cow.

"*What did he say?*" moaned Rex.

"Oink—Oink!" squealed Magnolia, realizing she lost her tiara in the scuffle.

"Get off of me, you pathetic cat!" scolded Sally-Mae.

Jake and Rex were lying flat on their backs, staring straight up into the grey-soaked sky while The Baron stood on the edge of the cliff, laughing himself silly. "Had enough, dear boy?"

"*I know I have,*" groaned Rex, in pain from the fall.

"What's that gibberish he keeps saying?" Jake thought out loud.

As Sally-Mae pushed Jake and Rex off her and Magnolia, she huffed, "And you call yourself the world's greatest detective? He said, '**Egonebay.**'" Jake and Rex still had a puzzled look on their faces.

"You know—**PIG LATIN**," she snapped, "the language of pigs! It doesn't take a rocket scientist to figure that out!"

"*What does it mean?*" barked Rex with Magnolia's tiara plopped on his head.

" '**Begone,**' you annoying cat!" she yelled.

"*Hey, listen, you over-the-hill beauty queen,*" he shouted. "*We're not going anywhere till you tell us what* '**Egonebay**' *means.*"

"**Begone!**" Sally-Mae screamed out, echoing to the top of the canyon, snatching Magnolia's tiara off of Rex's matted, furry head.

"*I told you when we met her, she was crazy!*" snickered Rex. "*She's been hanging around with that stupid pig for so long she's forgotten how to understand a simple question. We're not going away until you tell us what* '**Egonebay**' *means, once and for all!*"

"You can't be as dumb as you look," Sally-Mae glared at Rex. She then grabbed Magnolia's leash and dragged her off into the distance of the canyon in a huff. "And they say pigs aren't very smart."

"*I resemble that remark!*" hissed Rex.

"It's resent that remark, not resemble, you foolish fur ball," corrected Jake. "And the word, '**Egonebay**' actually means '**Begone!**' "

"*That's great!*" exclaimed Rex. "*Maybe you could use the same word with your magnifying glass and blast him to smithereens! Hey, how come a bolt of lightning didn't shoot out of your magnifying glass when you just said that word?*"

At Rex's question, Jake became filled with a sudden, overwhelming dread as he searched and searched his pockets for the magnifying glass. "Oh, no. I must have dropped it when we fell off the cliff."

Rex ran around terrified at the thought of the magnifying glass being lost. "*We're doomed!*"

"Yoo-hoo!" Snodgrass smirked from atop the cliff as Jake and Rex stared at him in a panic. "I believe your magnifying glass is right over there, dear boy!" He evilly pointed over to a large boulder a couple of yards from where Jake and Rex were standing.

"It's mine now!" Snodgrass yelled as he jumped off the cliff. His yellow linen cape-like coat blew open in the wind like a parachute as it floated him down the cliff. Rex's cat courage took hold as he sprang up onto the canyon ridge and made a soaring leap over to the magnifying glass, reaching it just before Snodgrass by a second. He hissed at the evil Baron as he flung the magnifying glass over to Jake.

Jake remembered the words Snodgrass used before to make his magnifying glass come to him. Not knowing exactly what he was saying, he commanded, "**Omecay otay emay.**" To his amazement, his magnifying glass flew right into the palm of his hand.

Irritated, and yet somewhat impressed, Snodgrass bellowed, "You learn fast, young Moustachio!"

"Faster than you think!" Jake answered with a confident grin. Rex ran for cover as Jake raised his magnifying glass and yelled out "**Egonebay!**"

Snodgrass's surprised eyes shot wide open as an earth-shattering ray of energy bolted out of Jake's magnifying glass. Jake flew backwards as the ray headed straight for Snodgrass. The bolt grazed the right side of his face singeing the blue handkerchief off his face and exposing the now-bleeding, jagged, *M* shaped scar.

The Baron became enraged with Jake's new found powers as he held his wounded face. "Your grandfather did this to me!" His maniacal screams echoed throughout the canyon. "You will pay for his foolishness!"

The reflections of Baily's beads from the solar eclipse were coming to an end. Alexa successfully traced the last few lines of the map onto her tracing paper. "I have it!" she exclaimed out loud. "I have the map!" Upon hearing the news, Sally-Mae, Magnolia, Bob Billy Bob, Rufus, Bernardo, Darlene, and Big Daddy came barreling towards her to snatch the map. Alexa and Sandy screamed in horror as the group got closer and closer with greed and determination in their eyes.

At that same moment, Jake and Rex also screamed out in fear as Snodgrass raised his magnifying glass, yelling out, **"Otay ouryay endway!"**

"Lexy!" Jake cried out. "We need more **TIME!**"

Alexa quickly searched her Inspector Girl backpack for the gift certificates they had gotten from The Librarian of Time.

"Hurry!" screamed Rex as another shock wave of energy blew out of Snodgrass's magnifying glass, headed directly for Jake.

With the crowd almost upon her, ready to snatch the map, and Jake about to be hit by the energy wave, Alexa ripped one of the certificates from the booklet and threw it into the air. It ignited in a blinding flash of light that spread across the canyon, freezing all in its path except Jake, Alexa, and Rex. Time had stopped, but only for a minute.

The bolt of lightning just hung there in mid-air right before Jake's eyes. "Run, Lexy!" he yelled out. "Run! We only have a few seconds!"

Alexa ran as fast as she could away from the treasure-hungry crowd with Sandy, frozen in time, stiffly bouncing around the backpack. She hid for her life behind an enormous banana yucca plant, still clutching the map tightly in her hands.

Escaping obliteration for that moment, Jake grabbed Rex and ran behind Snodgrass just as time fell back into place. The wave of energy exploded as it hit the spot where Jake had been standing. Snodgrass laughed contentedly, having thought he had just wiped Jake off the face of the planet.

"Yoo-hoo," smirked Jake from behind him. "Looking for me?"

"*You—!*" howled Snodgrass in a tyrannical fit of rage, realizing he'd just been outsmarted by Jake. "You're more trouble than your grandfather—*Is!*"

Jake quickly raised his magnifying glass and repeated Snodgrass's last phrase, "*Otay ouryay endway!*"

Realizing he was about to be zapped into oblivion, the Baron threw his own magnifying glass into the air and commanded, "*Eavelay isthay orldway!*"

It let out a burst of light as the vortex of wind hurled from its center. Jake's magnifying glass let out an array of flaming-red, deadly lightning bolts that just grazed the corner of Snodgrass's left leg.

The small, hidden, leather-bound book fell out of his boot as he leaped into his own magnifying glass, barely making his escape. "Fate can be very unexpected, young Moustachio. Till we meet again—" his evil voice echoed as he disappeared into the vortex. "Till we meet again!"

Snodgrass's magnifying glass exploded as it shrunk, disappearing into thin air from which it came.

CHAPTER NINETEEN
Follow The Map

A sigh of relief spread across Jake and Rex's faces as their heartbeats slowed down to a normal pace.

"*Is he gone?*" Rex asked, still shaking from the aftermath of the battle.

Jake hesitated a moment to catch his breath. He scanned the glowing horizon for any signs of his new-found nemesis. "I certainly hope he's gone. But I know he'll be back," he said.

"*How do you know?*"

Jake held his magnifying glass tightly in his hands as he caressed the gold metal rim and answered, "**I can feel it!**"

"***But for now—***" hesitated Rex.

A gigantic grin sprawled across Jake's mouth as his dimples deepened on his cheeks. "For now, my fine, furry friend, I think we're safe!" he exclaimed.

A tear of relief and joy dropped from the corner of Rex's left, golden eye as he jumped into Jake's arms and gave him a big, old, snuggly hug. "***You did it!***" he shouted thankfully.

"**We did it!**" declared Jake.

Rex noticed something odd blowing in the wind and scurried over to a bunch of cactuses to find what was left of the familiar, blue, handkerchief dangling from a tall, dark-green bush. He then tied it firmly around his fuzzy neck.

Suddenly, they heard the shriek of Alexa's voice as she screamed in terror. Big Daddy and the treasure-hunting posse descended upon the banana yucca plant where she and Sandy were hiding behind. She was surrounded as Sally-Mae, Bob Billy Bob, Rufus, Bernardo, Darlene, and Big Daddy loomed over her trying to grab the map from her tightly clenched hands. "Leave us alone!" she cried out. **"Leave us alone!"**

Jake and Rex ran as fast as they could to her side. "Leave her alone," Jake hollered angrily at the group.

"Yeah, he's got a loaded magnifying glass!" Rex warned.

Jake held up his magnifying glass, aimed it at the ruthless crowd, and announced, **"And I'm not afraid to use it!** Step away from the yucca plant and my sister, you vultures."

"And the guinea pig, too!" added Rex.

"Oh, you do care for Sandy, after all," sighed Jake.

"I thought it was a nice gesture," replied Rex.

Having just seen what Jake had done to Snodgrass, they all quickly backed away in fear from the yucca plant. Alexa and Sandy, with the map in hand, ran to join Jake and Rex.

"I thought we were goners for a minute there," she sighed with an exhausted breath, handing him the treasure map.

"Good job, Inspector Girl," he praised, giving her the warmest of hugs and a snappy high five. "It was a good thing we had those gift certificates!"

"I thought it was a nice touch!" purred Rex. *"The Moustachios rule!"*

"I sss—s—second that!" chutted Sandy.

"Wasn't stopping time the coolest thing ever!" shouted Alexa.

"It saved our butts!" declared Jake. "Thank heavens for Rupert and his certificates!"

"I can't wait to do it again," she added.

"*Ooooh—no!*" stuttered Rex. "*One time was more than enough for me! Besides, we'd have to be up to our ears in* **doo-doo** *again to have a need for one of those time-stopping certificates. And I, for one, have had enough* **doo-doo** *during this case to last me at least one of my nine lives!*"

As Jake and Alexa giggled at their crazy cat, they noticed the moon finishing the final last minutes of its journey over the sun. The eclipse ended, and the warmth of the sun radiated down upon them as its glow showered upon the red clay colored landscape of the canyon. Jake grabbed his magnifying glass and carefully studied the map, trying to make heads or tails of which trail to take to the treasure that awaited them.

"Where do we start, Jake?" asked Alexa, rummaging through her backpack for pink sunglasses for her and Sandy.

"It looks like we have to head up that ridge over there to the left of those four cactus plants," Jake explained.

"Now, wait just a doggone minute there, Inspector," bellowed Big Daddy, stomping his feet. "I hired y'all to find my cows and that map. The treasure is— *MINE!*"

Jake promised Big Daddy that any treasure they found would definitely belong to him. The crowd grumbled in disapproval, but hoping Big Daddy might share his new-found wealth, they reluctantly followed Big Daddy and the children up the ridge. Rufus cowardly tried to sneak away from the group. Big Daddy grabbed him by the neck, dragged him up the ridge, and reminded Rufus all the way that he would still pay for kidnapping his cows.

They hiked for quite a distance up a narrow dusty trail into the far reaches of the canyon. The temperature rose as the sun became fully visible after the eclipse.

"How much longer is this going to take?" snapped Sally-Mae. "It's almost time for Magnolia's nap. And if she doesn't get out of this dreadful sun, her precious piggly-wiggly pink skin is going to turn a dreadful shade of blotchy red."

Alexa rummaged through her backpack and pulled out a large bottle of sunblock. "This might help," she said, handing it to Sally-Mae.

Jake studied the sketch through his magnifying glass. As the sun's hot rays pierced the glass, it scorched the upper corner of the map. Alarmed, he quickly rubbed the corner before the soft, translucent paper containing Alexa's tracing disappeared in a puff of smoke. "Lexy," he asked, "are you sure you traced every part of the map from the cow's hide?"

Alexa scowled, tossed her hair back in a huff, and answered, "Of course, I did. I've been tracing for years! What's wrong?"

"With all those cows bantering, I can't concentrate! There's way too much moo-mooing here and moo-mooing there. Here a moo. There a moo. Everywhere a moo-moo," he complained.

Rex with a chuckle joined in with Sandy singing, "*Ee-i-ee-i-ooooooooo!*"

"Very funny. You two are quite the comedians," Jake sneered. "Maybe you two geniuses could explain why we seem to be walking around in circles."

"This is going to take us all day!" exclaimed Sally-Mae as she covered Magnolia's snout to curly tail with the sunblock.

"According to this map, we're standing right on top of the treasure," Jake explained.

"*Maybe someone took it!*" announced Rex.

"No—No—No," Jake analyzed, "my detective skills are telling me it's still here. I can feel it!"

"Give me that!" shouted Sally-Mae as she snatched the map from Jake's hands. She quickly scanned the map. "No wonder we're lost. You have this map upside down, you silly boy!"

"No, I don't!" exclaimed Jake in a fit of anger.

"Let me see that darn map!" barked Big Daddy, ripping it out of Sally-Mae's clutches. "You're both wrong. Ya' have it backwards!"

"No, it's not!" snapped Jake.

"*Let me take a look!*" interrupted Rex as he jumped up on top of Big Daddy's cowboy hat and snatched the map from his massive hands. "*Now, let me see!*"

"See what, you hair brain?" argued Jake. "Cats can't read!"

They all started tossing the map around, arguing who was right and who was wrong. Completely frustrated at having gotten this far without finding the treasure, Jake leaned against the stone wall kicking the orangey-red rock with the back of his foot. Suddenly, the stone wall rumbled and separated, leaving a narrow door-like opening. Jake immediately fell over backwards into the narrow crack behind him. As he stood up, the wall closed up, trapping him in the darkness.

"I think we need to go west," shouted Bob Billy Bob through everyone's loud arguing.

Turning her head towards Jake, Alexa asked, "What do you think, Jake?" She looked around in a panic, not being able to find him. "**Jake!**" she yelled. "**Jake! Where are you?**"

"**I'm in here!**" came his muffled reply.

"**Where?**" questioned Alexa as she put her ear up against the wall.

"Behind the wall," he explained. "**Kick it!**"

"*Kick what?*" asked Rex.

"The wall, you knucklehead—*THE WALL!*"

Everyone gathered close to the stone wall and started kicking it with all their might. Suddenly, the wall opened up again, and out popped Jake's head. "Hurry up before it closes. Everybody in," he ordered. "And, Lexy, grab your Inspector Girl flashlight. We're gonna need it!"

"*Are you nuts?*" cried out Rex. "*I'm not going in there. It's pitch black!*"

"Don't worry, Rexy Cat," said Alexa as Sandy handed her the flashlight. "I have my handy-dandy Inspector Girl flashlight!"

"*Well, I hope this time you checked your handy-dandy batteries!*" Rex snickered. "*The last time you tried to use that thing, it didn't work. And I wound up trapped on top of that ridiculous duck, flying through the darkness of the tunnels of The Museum of Time, looking for that stupid missing bell! I almost got killed!*"

"How many times do I have to tell you," growled Jake in frustration, "she was a goose, not a duck, you pesky pet!"

Jake reached through the crack in the wall and grabbed Rex by the fur of his neck pulling him in.

Alexa jumped in next, explaining, "That wasn't my fault. How was I supposed to know we would be creeping around a castle looking for stolen time with no lights?"

"Don't worry," exclaimed Sandy, "we packed extra double-life bbb—b—batteries!"

Magnolia waddled up to the narrow crack and tried to squeeze her porky self through. She let out a loud oink-oink here and an oink-oink there, crying out in Pig Latin, **"I'mway uckstay!"**

"What do you mean you're stuck?" cried Sally-Mae in disbelief. "Why, you're not an ounce over 300—I mean 100 pounds."

"What magical scale is she using!" laughed Rex. *"That pig is at least 400 pounds!"*

"Do you have any more of the sunblock lotion?" asked Jake.

"Of course I do," sighed Sally-Mae. "It's not polite to use up all of one's beauty products when one is borrowing them from a girlfriend!"

"Well," declared Jake, "lather up the pig and **push!**"

Sally-Mae poured the entire bottle of the lotion all over Magnolia's pink hide. She smelled like tropical coconut mixed with the smell of a dirty, old pig pen.

Rex immediately rustled through Alexa's backpack searching for some air freshener. With no luck, he cried, *"Hurry up, I'm dying in here!"*

With Magnolia all greased up, Sally-Mae, Bob Billy Bob, Rufus, and Big Daddy pushed on her squiggly, pig-tailed butt and shoved her through, squealing like the pig she was.

They all went tumbling through into the dark cavern, which held the mystery to the map deep within it. Knowing they would never fit through, Bernardo and Darlene just sat there happily holding each other's hooves with huge, endless smiles across their faces. While overlooking the cliffs of the canyon, they basked in the warmth of their bovine love.

CHAPTER TWENTY

The Treasure

Alexa flipped on her very pink Inspector Girl flashlight so they could get a good look at the cavern they had stumbled upon. From what they could see and the echoes from their voices, they knew it was massive in size. Suddenly, one by one, torches hanging in a circle on the stone walls surrounding them mysteriously lit up. Flames of fire illuminated the cave, streaming up to the ten-story-high, chiseled ceiling. At the top of the cavern was a hole that the smoke from the torches escaped from into the canyon air above. There were ancient Indian artifacts stacked up and hanging everywhere. Spread across the walls was a magnificent painted mural telling an ancient Indian story of a great battle. They all shivered as they heard haunting sounds of that battle radiating from the mural's wall into the sacred chamber.

"Where are we?" Alexa asked.

"This must be the ancient Indian burial ground that Chief Buffalo Hump was trying to tell Big Daddy about at the auction," surmised Jake as he studied every inch of the mural with his magnifying glass.

Painted on the walls were figures of Indians, some on horseback, fighting with what looked like an army of soldiers wearing fancy, blue uniforms with big, gold buttons. They carried rifles and swords of some kind that Jake did not recognize. One soldier was carrying a big, red flag with a blue *X* through it laced with white stars.

"An American Flag?" questioned Jake out loud. "No, it can't be—"

"What, Jake?" asked Alexa.

"I think that's a Confederate Flag from around the time of the Civil War!" exclaimed Jake.

"But why are they fighting the Indians?" huffed Rex.

"I don't recall learning about the Confederate Army ever being involved out west, let alone fighting with the Indians," said Alexa.

"Were there any battles between the Indians and the Confederate Army out here?" Jake asked Big Daddy.

Big Daddy took off his twenty-gallon black cowboy hat, scratched his head, shrugged his broad shoulders, and said, "I do recall some talk of a battle in these parts, but I never paid much mind to it. Those are just a bunch of tall tales ya' usually hear around a roaring camp fire in the dead of night. No one ever pays much attention to 'em! "

"I do remember from history class that towards the end of the Civil War more and more people came from the east to settle in the West," said Jake.

"And there was eventually a 'Gold Rush' out to California!" added Alexa.

"Well—" shouted Sally-Mae, "if I had someone barge into my pig parlor uninvited and kick me and my precious Magnolia out, I'd be madder than a dog with flees."

"With the Indian's land being taken over and their buffalo on the verge of extinction, they had no choice but to fight!" declared Rufus.

"By the looks of this painting," announced Rex, *"that's exactly what they did!"*

"But this can't be all there is to the treasure!" barked Big Daddy.

They all agreed as they went scavenging wildly through the vastness of the cavern, greedily searching for the treasure. Jake, Alexa, and Rex just stood there watching them make a ridiculous spectacle of themselves. Out of nowhere, Jake heard a fluttering high up in the ceiling. He looked up and saw the light-brown hawk flying around in circles near the opening the smoke from the torches was still blowing out of. It was almost as if the hawk was trying to tell him something by its unusual pattern of flight. Jake quickly combed the area for clues with Alexa and Rex trailing close behind.

"What are you looking for, Jake?" Alexa and Rex questioned.

"I'm not sure, but when I find it—I'll know it!"

Leaving nothing to chance, he examined every inch of the mural again with the magnifying glass, as a world-class detective would. "**AHHH——HAAA!**" he shouted. "Very clever!" Painted on the Indian Chief's arm of the mural was a tattoo of the light brown hawk. Jake felt around the Indian Chief's tattoo and watched in amazement as the mural split into two. The now opened wall revealed a hidden chamber filled with *the treasure!*

Everyone came running over, stunned at the uncountable sacks and sacks of over–flowing, gold-colored coins.

With her crystal-clear-blue eyes mesmerized by what she saw, Sally-Mae shouted, "*Magnolia—we're rich!*"

"We sure are, sugar-pie!" exclaimed Rufus.

"I second that!" yelled Bob Billy Bob.

"What do you mean, 'We're rich'?" snarled Big Daddy

as he started to grab the sacks one by one. The weight of the coins tore through the aged leather sacks as the coins poured out to the dusty ground. Big Daddy dropped to his knees as he feverishly tried to reclaim his loot. "***This money belongs to me!***"

"There's more than enough here for all of us to share," snapped back Sally-Mae.

"***Eahyay!***" snorted Magnolia.

"You'll never be able to get all that money out of here without our help anyway," explained Rufus.

"You expect me to share my good fortune after ya' kidnapped my cows, ya' yella'-belly scallywag! I'd rather sit here for the rest of my natural born days than share my loot with the likes of you!" grumbled Big Daddy.

Jake bent down to help pick up the fallen coins. His eyelashes tickled as they brushed up against the frame of the magnifying glass. He then squinted to examine closely one of the gold coins. Being a young coin collector, Jake had read many books about the history of coins throughout the world. He noticed an Indian man on the face of the coin and a buffalo on the back. Except for being much bigger in size and gold, it looked exactly like a buffalo nickel. But this coin was stamped 1856S with the words "United States of America" circling around the Indian's head and "One Dollar" under the buffalo.

Jake scratched the back of his neck in confusion. He knew that during that time period a man by the name of James Longacre designed almost all of the money. Coins were minted on the east coast of the country, and they were also made out west in San Francisco. That explains why the coins were

stamped 'S'. But how, he thought, did all this money end up stashed in this canyon? And why? The main dollar around the time of the Civil War was a large Indian head-type gold dollar. But not this one! It had a woman on the front, not a man.

How could this be? The only coin with an Indian and a buffalo on it that Jake could recall was the famous "Buffalo Nickel," which was designed by a guy named James Fraser in 1912, years after the Civil War!

Things were strange on this side of the magnifying glass, but not this strange! Are events of time from both worlds the same or different? He wondered. Could it be that history on one side of the magnifying glass is different from the other? And could people in one world alter time and events in the other?

Alexa came running over to join them in picking up the coins, "Wow!" she exclaimed. "This is the biggest buffalo nickel I've ever seen!"

"That's exactly what I was thinking," replied Jake as he continued to rummage through the pile, examining each and every coin he could.

Suddenly, the hawk that was soaring high above them let out a loud screech and swooped down, circling right above their heads. He came to rest on Jake's right shoulder. Everyone was motionless in fear as Jake stood frozen, also too terrified to move.

"Someone do something," he whispered in a panic.

"Hey you, annoying cat," yelled Sally-Mae, trying to

swoosh the gigantic bird away with her pink silk scarf, "aren't you supposed to go chasing after birds or something?"

They all looked down at him with great expectations in their eyes.

"Are you all crazy? Have ya' seen the size of that thing?" cried Rex cowardly. *"Here, birdie, birdie! Here, birdie, birdie!"*

"Well, that's not going to do anything," snapped Sally-Mae.

The hawk started pecking at Jake's head, **"Ouch!"** he cried. **"Stop that!"**

Alexa frantically waved her arms in the air as she fearlessly stomped right up to Jake and his new-found friend. **"Sheeeeew, you mean old bird! Leave him alone!"**

The hawk flapped his wings in a wild fit of rage and squawked out loud at the group.

"Well, that's just down-right rude!" complained Sally-Mae. "Isn't it, Magnolia?"

"Eryvay uderay!" snorted Magnolia.

The magnificent, yet stubborn, hawk took flight and flew right through the crowd, sending them diving for cover among the sacks of coins. He came to rest on top of an old, tattered, Indian headdress. A bright-red glow started to emanate from it. Years of age and wear started to vanish from the headdress until it appeared new. The majestic headdress was woven with beautiful, bright, orange, red, and white feathers. Horse hair hung from the tips of the feathers, and elaborate beading glistened from the head band in front. Colorful rosettes with rabbit tails dangled from each side.

As the hawk suddenly disappeared into the haze, the cavern began to rumble. The flames from the torches blew out, and the ground beneath their feet shook as if they were standing on a sea of Jell-O. The ancient Indian artifacts started to fall from the walls as pieces of the stone came crumbling down.

"What is that?" shrieked Rufus, snatching a few coins into his pockets before burying his head under a sack of money.

"It's a darn earthquake!" bellowed Big Daddy as he jumped around in the confusion, looking for a way out.

Jake and Alexa dove into the pile of coins to protect themselves from falling debris. Rex grabbed Alexa's Inspector Girl backpack with Sandy inside and ran for cover, barely escaping a falling boulder. Bob Billy Bob sprang into the air, pushing Sally-Mae and Magnolia away from a collapsing wall. Big Daddy, unable to find an exit, slid under a pile of buffalo skins and hid for his life.

"*Would this be an appropriate time to say it?*" screamed Rex.

"Now would be as best as any!" Jake yelled out.

"*We're doomed!*" bellowed Rex from under the rubble. "*Doomed, I tell ya'!*"

Within a few minutes the ground began to settle as the rumbling and shaking of the earth came to an abrupt stop. There was a moment of dead silence as the torches lit up once again, one by one. They all waited before getting up to make sure it would be safe.

"Y'all O.K.!" hollered Big Daddy through the thick dust floating in the air.

"Magnolia's not all right!" sobbed Sally-Mae.

They all ran to Sally-Mae and Magnolia's side to see what had happened. "Look at her," she cried, tears rolling down her face. "*Just look at my baby!*"

"Is she hurt?" asked Alexa, putting her backpack on.

"The pain is just too unbearable for me to take," moaned Sally-Mae.

"What's wrong?" Jake demanded.

Sally-Mae fell hopelessly to the ground crying in utter devastation, "**Magnolia's tiara is broken! It's smashed to smithereens!**"

They all breathed a sigh of relief, rolling their eyes in exasperation at the ridiculousness of the pig's broken tiara, but also thankful that they all lived through the quake.

Jake heard a rustling coming from the other side of the cave. "What's that sound?"

"*It's probably that overgrown bird,*" suggested Rex as he wiped the dust from his eyes with his paw.

All their attention turned to the sound echoing through the thick, dusty air. Slow footsteps drew nearer to the group as they held their breaths in nervous anticipation of what was going to happen next. Out from the cloud of dust came a tall, old-looking man wearing a colorful buckskin shirt with fringe dangling from his sleeves. He had on brown, animal skin pants and tall, leather, boot-like moccasins on his feet. Adorned on his head was the same headdress that the hawk had landed on prior to the quake.

They all gasped in disbelief when Big Daddy angrily yelled out, "That's the guy from the auction, the one who sold me those darn cows. That's Chief Buffalo Hump!"

"So—this mystery unravels," Jake mumbled under his breath.

CHAPTER TWENTY-ONE

The Mystery Unraveled

Jake bent down and picked up a fallen feather from the hawk as he approached Chief Buffalo Hump. "I believe you dropped this!" he announced with a satisfied grin, waving it in the dusty air.

The group looked shocked and confused.

"What do ya' mean, he dropped the feather?" barked Big Daddy.

"Just what I said," explained Jake. "This feather fell off the hawk when he swooped over our heads."

"But that would mean—," started Alexa.

"*That he's the hawk!*" finished Rex.

"Exactly, my good pussycat, exactly!" Jake grinned.

"You've been flying around us ever since we got here," declared Jake, confidence oozing from his voice. "Haven't you?"

"Truth can be seen with the eyes and spoken from the heart, young one," answered Chief Buffalo Hump. "The Great Spirit has answered my call in bringing you here to my side."

"What is it that you want from us?" Jake asked.

"For the honor of my people to be **restored**," he answered.

Jake scratched his head, perplexed at Chief Buffalo Hump's answer. "Restored? I don't understand."

"History has been unkind to my people. It has been told that we were thieves and dishonorable warriors. The truth lies before you," he said, pointing to the mural. "A great battle was fought outside these sacred walls between my brave sons and the army of blue soldiers."

"You were fighting with the Confederate Army, weren't you?" Jake asked.

Chief Buffalo Hump nodded yes.

"But why?" questioned Alexa.

"My tribesmen were good men. They helped guide many frontiersmen through these lands as they laid the route from the East to the West called the Butterfield Trail. We were responsible for its success, but long forgotten in time."

"That trail became the Butterfield Overland Express!" exclaimed Jake. "Our great-great-grandma Moustachio's dad was one of the mailmen who used this route."

"And that trail eventually became the foundation for the transcontinental railroads," added Big Daddy.

"I met a very important man on this trail traveling a long journey to the West accompanied by his daughter. She told of her father's great job to design currency for this new land," said Chief Buffalo Hump.

"That must have been James Longacre and his daughter," explained Jake. "He must have been on his way to work at the San Francisco Mint. Wait a second—" he continued as he rummaged through his pockets looking for the Indian head penny he found earlier that day. "Around 1858, Longacre designed this Indian head penny. Most people think it's an Indian on the face of this coin. But I read it might actually be Longacre's daughter wearing an Indian headdress given to her by an Indian chief while her Dad was sketching her face to put on the penny!"

"Truth speaks from you, my son," said Buffalo Hump.

"No way!" smirked Rex. *"You're— him?"*

"So that means that the headdress you're wearing and this one on the penny— are the same!" exclaimed Alexa.

"My warriors and I stayed by his side, protecting his safe passage through this treacherous land. In gratitude for our protection of his daughter, he honored my people by using my image on his new coin."

Jake bent over and picked up one of the gold dollars with Chief Buffalo Hump's face on it. "But this coin doesn't exist in any of our history books, at least on my side of the magnifying glass."

"The coins were never used," he explained. "A great war of freedom was about to explode across this land."

"The Civil War!" shouted Alexa.

"My warriors fought a long battle protecting this gold on its way east along the trail. We were attacked for our supplies, horses, and the gold. But my men protected this gold with their lives. Upon leaving this canyon, we were ambushed by renegade troops. My people did not survive."

"How sss—s—sad," chutted Sandy.

"History has told that the Comanches took the gold and fled into the hills. The secret of our great battle and the truth lie here in this cavern. The gold was hidden here where the renegade troops would not find it. The battle marked for all time on these walls. And the path to our sacred burial ground painted on the hide of our most sacred of cows only to be revealed when the pale moon rises in front of the sun god."

"A total solar eclipse," stated Jake.

"And the last time that happened—" Jake started to explain.

"Was when Great-Great-Grandma Mary's father was delivering the mail for The Butterfield Overland Express—" continued Alexa.

"*But during that eclipse, the wind blew so hard his mail flew all over the canyon—*" added Rex.

"He never got the chance to read the treasure mmm—m—map on the cow's hide," chutted Sandy, "and find the treasure."

"And the mystery remained buried deep within this canyon until now," finished Jake. "That's why you've been following us. You wanted to make sure we unraveled this mystery before the eclipse passed."

"Now my people can rest as they join the Spirit God in the heavens. And I will join them once you return this gold to its rightful owners and our honor is restored."

"What do you mean 'return this gold?'" demanded Big Daddy as he stomped his feet in a fit of rage. "You sold me those darn cows and promised that treasures would await me at the end of my journey. Well, the doggone journey's over, and this gold here belongs to me!"

"The treasures that the Spirit God will bestow upon you does not necessarily lie within the sacks of gold, Big One," warned the Chief.

"So—let me get this straight," pondered Sally-Mae. "Since we all led to the discovery of these coins in this dusty, old cave, which, by the way, you really need to dust once in a while, and since no one gets the gold, does this mean that treasures will fall upon all of us, or just Big Daddy?"

"Why you backstabbin', pig lover!" snarled Big Daddy

at Sally-Mae.

"It was just a simple, little, old question," she said. "You don't have to get all huffy about it!"

"The Spirit God will bestow treasures upon those who honor my people," explained Chief Buffalo Hump.

"And to those who don't?" questioned Rufus, fiddling with the coins he snatched earlier in his pockets.

Suddenly, the cave began to shake as if another quake was about to occur. "The wrath of the Spirit God will curse those with eternal bad luck!" he warned.

"Well, then," declared Jake. "This gold must be returned to the place it came from, the U.S. Mint, and the history of the coins' disappearance corrected."

Big Daddy just stood there all grumpy having lost all that gold.

"What do you think they'll do with it, Jake?" asked Alexa.

"They'll probably put it in a museum—I guess."

Chief Buffalo Hump thanked them for honoring the Comanche people as he prepared to leave. He turned to Jake, placing his hand warmly on his head. A glow of light emanated from it as he said, "The purest of thoughts and heart lie within you, my son. Use the gifts you've been given wisely as your destiny unfolds!"

Jake gave the chief a grateful smile as he thanked him and promised him that he would.

"May the Spirit God bless you all with the treasures of life's happiness and good fortune."

"Oh, one more thing!" exclaimed Jake as he purposely searched his pockets for a buffalo nickel. With no luck, he quickly turned to Alexa and asked her if she had any buffalo nickels in her Inspector Girl backpack. Alexa searched and searched. Finally, Sandy found one in Alexa's spare money pocket in the right-hand corner of the backpack. Jake grabbed it and waved it in the air, showing it to the chief, and asked, "How did your face end up on the buffalo nickel? It was minted almost fifty years after the Civil War."

The chief smiled, gave him a wink, and said, "Some mysteries are best left unsolved, my son." And with that said, Chief Buffalo Hump transformed himself into the hawk and soared up the heights of the cavern, flying right out of the opening at the top into the sun-drenched sky.

"*How do you think his face got on that nickel?*" asked Rex.

"The man on the face of the buffalo nickel was made up from three different sketches of three different Indian chiefs back in 1912," explained Jake.

"Maybe Chief Buffalo Hump was one of the three chiefs sketched," suggested Alexa.

"YYY—Y—Yeah!" exclaimed Sandy.

"Or maybe fate corrected time!" pondered Jake.

"*What do you mean?*" questioned Rex.

"If these gold dollars were meant to be, then that would mean Chief Buffalo Hump and his people were meant to be part of our history. A twist of fate changed that from happening when the coins were lost. Maybe the three Indian chiefs sketched by Fraser, when combined wound up looking like Chief Buffalo Hump. Maybe this is fate's way of correcting a wrong and at long last honoring the Comanches by having Chief Buffalo Hump's face finally end up on a coin, the buffalo nickel," suggested Jake.

They all stood there smiling at the thought and, of

course, at Jake's world-class detective skills.

Suddenly, the ground began to vibrate wildly one final time. The rumble of the Earth echoed throughout the cavern.

"It's another quake," yelled Big Daddy. "Save yourselves!"

"*Ohhhh—Noooo!*" warned Rex. "*Not again!*"

Scrambling frantically to once again save their lives, they dove under the pile of coins for protection.

"We're going to die!" cried Rufus cowardly as he once again greedily tried to stuff more coins into his pockets.

The walls started to shake and shudder when one massive explosion blew out the far wall of the cave, giving them an exit back out to the canyon. The bright sunlight poured in, causing the gold to glow so brilliantly it illuminated the dark cavern.

"Well, I reckon we best get these sacks of money outta' here," declared Big Daddy.

"I'll help!" suggested Rufus with a foolish grin.

"I don't think so," observed Jake in an accusatory tone. "And you just might want to empty out your pockets."

"Rufus McGraw, did you steal some of that money?" scolded Sally-Mae.

Rufus just stood there with a guilty look as he reluctantly emptied his pockets. "But sugar-pie!" he murmured.

"Don't you sugar-pie me! Just wait till Mama gets home," she warned. "You're going to get an ear full! Why, I wouldn't be surprised if you'll be sleeping out in the barn!"

"*More like sleeping in a jail cell!*" exclaimed Rex.

"So how are we going to get all this money out of here?" Alexa asked as she rummaged through her backpack for a hair brush.

"Well, let's go fetch us some of my cows, and we can hitch the bags to 'em and carry them right outta' here," suggested Big Daddy as he led them out of the cave.

"It'll be a beautiful parade of pink, brown, and white going down the canyon," declared Sally-Mae, excitedly as she looked down at the endless rows of cows mooing at the base of the canyon. "We can pretend it's a rehearsal for my wedding march. Magnolia will lead; you know, she's gonna to be my maid-of-honor."

"*You must be kidding me!*" Rex snickered. "*You want us to practice for your wedding march with all those cows carrying the money out of here and that stupid pig leading the way?*"

"You know, Mr. Pussy Cat," she spat. "**I don't like you!** You are not invited to my wedding, after all!"

"*Quick, get a dust pan and a broom to scoop up my broken heart!*" shouted Rex, collapsing in hysterical laughter on the dusty ground.

"Rexy Cat, be nice!" reminded Alexa.

"I like you," Sally-Mae said, pointing to Alexa. "And, of course, your pretty little guinea pig. You appreciate the beauty in all animals, especially pigs."

"Hey—what about me?" demanded Jake. "I like pigs! Can't I come to the wedding?"

"I haven't decided about you, Inspector," snapped Sally-Mae. "After all, you did unjustly accuse me of stealing Big Daddy's cows. Now, didn't you?"

"True," answered Jake. "But I wasn't that far off. After all, your father is the guilty one!"

Big Daddy stomped over to Jake as they both looked

happily down at the cow filled canyon. Slapping him hard on his back he praised, "Well, my boy, ya' did it! Ya' solved the case, got my cows back, and found the treasure. Ya' really are a world class detective!"

"*I'm starving,*" groaned Rex. "*Can we go home now?*"

"Rex, we really should help return the gold," answered Jake.

"Don't ya' worry yourself, Inspector," Big Daddy announced cheerfully. "I'll make sure the money is returned and the story of the Comanche Indians is told to the whole world!"

"Are you sure?" Jake asked.

"I promise!" he vowed.

"Well, I am a little hungry, and we do have a family barbeque to get back to," replied Jake.

"Me, too!" confessed Alexa. "I can't wait until Daddy fires up the barbeque and starts cooking some hamburgers, hot dogs, and especially spareribs."

"*I just love your dad's spareribs!*" announced Rex, licking his whiskers.

"Me, ttt—t—too!" chutted Sandy.

Unexpectedly, from out of the bright light of the sun, the hawk returned soaring over their heads clutching something tightly with his claws. It was a small, rolled-up piece of paper that he dropped down from the sky. The paper gently floated its way down. When it got close enough, Alexa snatched it right up from its mid-air flight.

"What's that?" Sandy questioned, looking over Alexa's shoulders from the top of the backpack.

Alexa unraveled the paper. Her big, blue eyes grew enormous as she stared in amazement at the flowery dots over the beautifully written "I's."

"It's—It's—Great-Great-Grandma Mary's letter," she stuttered.

"What letter?" Jake asked with a curious grin.

"It's the other half of the letter that Great-Great-Grandma Mary wrote to her sister. You remember, the one with the rest of the barbeque sauce recipe written on it."

Alexa handed Jake the missing half of the letter, which he closely scanned with his magnifying glass. "Well, what do you know—it is the other half of the letter!" Jake turned over the aged sheet of paper and found the rest of the hand-drawn sketch that Great-Great-Grandma Mary's father drew in order to find Chief Buffalo Hump.

Rex had a huge smile sprouting under his whiskers *"Now, what do you suppose really happened back then?"* he asked with cat-like curiosity.

"I don't know," confessed Jake, "but I'd bet my magnifying glass it was quite a misadventure!"

"Well, after all," giggled Alexa, "mysterious misadventures do run in the family! So what's the missing barbeque sauce ingredient anyway?"

Jake quickly read through the rest of the letter and declared, "**MOLASSES!** It's two cups of molasses!"

"Molasses!" bellowed Big Daddy. "Now why didn't I think of that? That's exactly what I need to add to my own barbeque sauce recipe to make it doggone perfect. Why, with that in it, I'm gonna to be the biggest barbeque sauce king there ever was and will ever be!"

"See," Jake grinned. "You did the right thing by deciding to return the gold, and already good fortune has come your way."

Big Daddy took off his twenty-gallon cowboy hat, scratched his head, thought for a minute. "Well, I reckon you're right!"

"He always is!" nodded Alexa.

"*Annoyingly so, I might add!*" Rex smirked.

"After all," chutted Sandy, "he is *The Great Inspector Jake Moustachio!*"

Jake passed the letter to Alexa who then very carefully folded it and placed it into the front left pocket of her pants.

"Well, I reckon this is goodbye, Inspector," gushed Big Daddy.

"What about Rufus?" Jake asked.

"Oh, don't ya' worry yourself about him. I'll make sure he gets what's coming to him." Big Daddy firmly shook Jake's hand and then gave Alexa a tender kiss on her head. "Take care partner, and you, too, little lady."

"Say good-bye to Bernardo for us," Alexa fondly murmured.

"I sure will do that," he called out as he walked away. "Ya' know—ya' got yourselves some fine animals there."

The children smiled with such pride at Rex and Sandy. Big Daddy then demanded everyone to follow him around the ridge to help find Bernardo and Darlene. They all then went down to the base of the canyon to start gathering up the rest of the cows. Alexa just stood there with the cutest grin emerging across her face.

"What's so funny?" Jake asked.

"Just look at all those **pink** cows!" she giggled.

"*Yeah, that's a lot of* **pink** *milk!*" Rex snickered.

"Sandy, sweetie, can you see all this from my **pink** backpack?"

"The sun's glaring in my eyes. Let me grab my **ppp— p—pink** sunglasses," chutted Sandy.

Jake tried to hold back a smile, but it was no use. "Very funny, you guys. I suppose you'll be telling me next that a black and white cow makes cookies and cream milk!"

"You never know," they laughed. *"You never know!"*

Jake, Rex, and Alexa carrying Sandy followed a different trail, which led them back down to the spot that was covered with the many yucca plants.

"You know, you owe me a Clunky Chunky Chocolate Bar," reminded Rex.

"I remember, Rexy Cat," said Alexa. "Mommy promised to get some at the store. I'm sure she didn't forget."

As they continued down the trail, Rex slipped on something squishy. "Wooooow," he screamed, falling flat on his furry butt.

"Are you O.K.?" the children yelled out.

"I slipped on something."

"Rex, we're not cleaning you up again if you stepped in doo-doo," scolded Jake.

"It wasn't doo-doo. It was something else!"

Jake grabbed his magnifying glass and searched the ground for the object Rex slipped on. "What's this?" he questioned, reaching under the corner of one of the banana yucca plants. It was a small, dirt-covered, leather-bound book.

Alexa and Rex came running over. "What did you find?" they asked.

"This must be Snodgrass's book," he declared. "You guys remember, the one that Big Daddy said was slipped into Snodgrass's boot.

"Well, how did that end up here?" Alexa questioned.

"It must have fallen out of his boot when he made his escape into his magnifying glass," declared Jake.

"He's going to be awfully mmm—m—mad when he finds out he lost it!" exclaimed Sandy.

"And even madder when he finds out we have it!" Rex announced, trembling in fear.

Jake began to flip through the book, trying to figure out why it was so important to Snodgrass. The tattered pages were filled with jumbled words that Jake had never seen before. "What language do you guys suppose this is?" he asked as he showed them the book.

Alexa couldn't make heads or tails of the words either. "Maybe it's a diary of some sort, possibly written in Egyptian," she said, trying to think of an answer to the dilemma.

"Wait a second!" Jake exclaimed. "Snodgrass was yelling in Pig Latin to get his magnifying glass to work."

"Do you think they are commands to work the magnifying glasses?"

Jake anxiously rummaged through the pages of the book. Finding nothing there to help answer their questions, he decided to hold up his magnifying glass, shouting, "There's only one way to find out!"

Alexa, Sandy, and Rex screamed at the top of their voices, "**WAIT!**"

"What's wrong?"

"Are you crazy?" Rex shouted. *"You just can't go willy-nilly yelling out commands in a language you don't understand yet!"*

"Yeah, Jake, you could get us all killed!" scolded Alexa.

"Or ddd—d—destroy the universe or something!" chutted Sandy nervously.

Jake had to agree with them. It would be awfully dangerous and slightly irresponsible. *Dad always says you should always understand how something works before you use it!* "O.K., we'll wait and decode the book before we try out any of the commands, assuming these are commands, after all!"

Alexa asked Sandy to dig for a wipey so she could clean off the dirt on the brown, leather cover. Sandy searched and searched, finally popping out of the backpack with a container of disinfectant wipes. Alexa vigorously scrubbed some of the cover clean and, to everyone's surprise, revealed the word **Oustachiomay!**

"Now what do you suppose this means?" she asked in amazement.

"Well, it can't be that hard to decode one word," reasoned Jake. "Let's see, you take the first letter of the word and move it to the end."

"Then you add **'ay'** or **'way'** to the end of that," recalled Alexa.

"*So, if you were doing that backwards you would get—*"

Their eyes lit up in shock as the decoded word finally made perfect sense. They all screamed out loud in utter confusion—"***MOUSTACHIO!***"

"Quick, Lexy, clean the rest of the cover!" urged Jake. "There has to be more!"

Alexa feverishly scrubbed and scrubbed the rest of the cover to reveal another word before "Moustachio." It was "***Uckbay***," which they quickly translated into—***BUCK,*** their grandfather's first name.

"***Grandpa!***" they shouted.

"This book is Grandpa's." announced Jake.

"But how did Snodgrass get it?" questioned Alexa.

"And why did he keep it so close to him?" added Rex.

"I'll tell you why," explained Jake as he flipped through the pages. "Grandpa must have spent years figuring out how to get the magnifying glass to work. He probably wrote the commands in Pig Latin to make it as difficult as possible for anyone else to figure out. Snodgrass must have gotten hold of the book and somehow decoded all or at least some of the commands."

"That evil, treacherous villain used your own grandfather's words against us!" Rex exclaimed.

"Well, two can play at that game. And we'll be ready for him the next time he decides to pop up out of thin air," Jake promised.

"This book is filled with thousands and thousands of tiny words," warned Alexa. "It'll take us forever to decode everything."

"Then we better get home and get to work!" Jake concluded as he tucked the book safely into his back pocket.

"I wonder how long Snodgrass has had the book?" pondered Alexa.

"It looks like we have our very own mystery to solve!" suggested Rex as he curiously stroked his wiry whiskers.

Sandy shook with excitement over the possibility of a new, mysterious case to solve. She popped right out of the backpack and shouted, "Oh, boy! A mystery! We need to get someone to help us with this case. Like a bbb—b—bunch of sleuths or something!"

They all turned and looked at her with exasperation on

their annoyed faces. "Sweetie," Alexa sighed. "We are the sleuths. Remember—Moustachio Investigations: *Solving Mysteries Is Our Specialty!*"

"Oh, yeah!" she thought out loud with a glimmer of clarity. "I forgot!"

"You really do need to start writing some of this stuff down," suggested Alexa.

"*Why bother? Pig face will only forget where she left the crayons and the notepad anyway!*" sneered Rex.

"For the hundredth time, I'm not a **Pig!** I am a **Princess Guinea Pig** from **PERU**, you common alley cat!"

"*I resemble that remark,*" Rex yelled out with a devilish grin.

"It's 'resent,' you loony fur ball. How many times do I have to tell you the word is not 'resemble,' it's 'resent!' " corrected Jake.

"*Ya' don't have to get all huffy!*" Rex mumbled.

"Listen, you two," scolded Jake, "if you guys don't stop fighting, I'm going to send you to your rooms for a time-out the moment we get home."

"*We don't have any rooms. The pig lives in a stinky, old cage covered with food, right next to where she doos, what she doos. I, on the other hand, am a domesticated animal of the highest pedigree. I get to roam freely among the family members whenever I want!*"

"Well," ordered Jake, "if you two don't stop fighting, Rex, you'll be living in your own cage, eating where you doo what you doo—*TOO!*"

"Now kiss and make up!" suggested Alexa, trying to push them together.

"***Ewwwww!***" they both cried out in disgust.

199

Jake was exhausted from dealing with his two squabbling pets. "All right," he coaxed, "how about paw shakes, and we'll call it even." Rex and Sandy reluctantly decided to call a temporary truce and shook paws.

Jake glanced up at the canyon with a worried look. His hand grasped the magnifying glass tightly as he remembered his battle with Snodgrass and all the weird things he said.

"What's the matter, Jake?" Alexa asked.

"Snodgrass said that Grandpa gave him that jagged scar on his face."

"*You mean the one shaped like an M,*" stated Rex.

"I wonder how that happened, and when?"

Alexa went over to her brother and gave him a comforting hug, "Well, whatever happened, it looks like Grandpa put up quite a fight!"

"*Just like you did, Inspector!*" Rex exclaimed with an enormous amount of pride. "*Your grandpa would be very proud of you, both of you!*"

Jake just stood there, still sad and droopy.

"What's wrong, Jake? You were amazing when you dueled with Snodgrass." Alexa recalled. "You solved the mystery, saved the cows, and found the treasure!"

"*Not to mention restored the honor of the Comanche Indians!*" added Rex.

"I—I know," he stuttered. "But—didn't—Snodgrass say that—I was more trouble than Grandpa —*Is?*"

"*So—?*"

" '*Is*' is a present tense verb. '*Was*' a past tense verb, would have been the correct choice of word."

"Well, the '*Is*' really doesn't make much sense then," thought Alexa. "Does it?"

"Maybe that evil man never went to school and never learned about those verbie words," suggested Sandy.

"There is always that possibility, sweetie," surmised Alexa. "And the word is verb: a word that characteristically is the grammatical center of a predicate and the expression of an act."

"*Nice definition!*" purred Rex.

"Jake's not the only smart Moustachio, you know!" she exclaimed. "Inspector Girl's got a few tricks up her sleeve, too!"

Jake gave his sister a nudge and declared, "I couldn't have solved the case without ya'!"

Rex and Sandy started clearing their throats waiting for a compliment.

"And you two pesky pets, too!" he added. "But I still think Snodgrass knew exactly what he was saying."

"*Listen, he probably was just trying to get your goat. There was a lot going on. You had those crazy lunatics chasing Alexa and pig breath over there. You had the solar eclipse going on, not to mention all those lightning bolts flying around here. Maybe you misunderstood what he said,*" explained Rex, jumping oddly up and down.

"True, there was a lot going on, but I'm pretty sure I heard him say '*Is*,' "declared Jake.

Rex crossed his back legs and continued jumping around like he had ants in his pants. "*Can we save the grammar lesson for later. I think I need to go!*" he winced.

"Stop jumping around, you pesky hair ball. We're going!" yelled Jake.

"*No, I mean, I really, really have to go!*" he moaned.

"Well, there's plenty of yucca plants around here. Go

behind one of them." Jake smirked.

"*I will not. Do I look like I was raised in a barn? I'm a domesticated animal, not one of those disgusting cows of Big Daddy's or one of those sickening goats who freely **doo** what they **doo** any old place at the Giddy Goat Ranch. That's what a litter box is for!*"

The children broke out laughing themselves silly over Rex's predicament. Rex was happy to finally see Jake's worried face vanish behind his handsome smile.

"All right!" Jake chuckled. "We're going."

Jake held his magnifying glass firmly in his right hand and then swung it over his shoulder, towards the sun-drenched sky over the canyon, shouting out, "**Omehay**," Pig Latin for "**Home.**"

The magnifying glass soared through the air as an enormous bolt of lightning shot out of it. It hung suspended in mid-air, growing larger and larger. A vortex of wind tunneled out, blowing tumbleweed and yucca plants all around the dusty clay-colored ground.

"**Nice** *job!*" called out Rex through the wind. "*Using a little **PIG LATIN** to command the magnifying glass, **sweet!***"

"Who's going first?" called out Jake.

Rex, having to **go** really, really badly, pushed everyone out of the way. "*Don't forget, it's one meow for yes and two meows for no! Thank your mother for the new cat litter; it smells much, much better. And you owe me four cans of cat food. Well, really only three because I shouldn't have brought the fourth can, but it was a good thing I did because we would have been goners, and—*"

"Would you **jump** already, you foolish feline?" demanded Jake.

"*I'm going—I'm going,*" Rex growled. He then took a deep breath with an enormous leap into the magnifying glass's tunnel of wind, yelling, "**My litter box awaits!**"

Alexa then gave Sandy a kiss and a little snuggle before scooting her to the bottom of the Inspector Girl backpack.

"Thanks for letting me ttt—t—tag along!" Sandy chutted. "LLL—L—Love ya'!"

"Any time, sweetie, any time," said Alexa. "Love you, too! Hold on tight, the ride gets a little bumpy." With that said, she grabbed the missing half of the letter from her left pants pocket and stashed it in the secret compartment of her Inspector Girl backpack before zipping it and Sandy up, all safe and sound. "I can't wait to show Grandma the missing letter! She's going to be so excited I found the missing ingredient. Now she can make her barbeque sauce!"

"Lexy," warned Jake. "You can't give her that letter!"

"Why not?"

"How are you going to explain where you got it?" he reminded, crinkling his nose.

"Well, I didn't really think about that!" she agreed. "You know I'm not an adult!"

"**LEXY!**" he scolded.

"Oh, all right," she said. "Don't worry, I'll think of something. I promise she'll **never** know where I really got it from!"

She grabbed her brother's hand tightly, gave him a warm and slightly naughty smile, and they all jumped into the magnifying glass, happy to be returning home.

CHAPTER TWENTY-TWO

Dad's Barbeque!

Faster and faster the young detectives slid towards home. Twisting and turning around with every bend inside the vortex. Twinkles of color exploded as they shot right out of the magnifying glass, tumbling over each other onto the granite floor of their bathroom. The tunnel of wind came to an abrupt stop. The magnifying glass, dangling in mid-air, let out a final explosion of light as Jake extended his right arm, opened up his hand and commanded, "***Omecay otay emay!***" The magnifying glass willingly obeyed, flying right to him.

"Is it me, or was that ride just a little extra bumpy?" Jake smirked, rubbing his sore butt before placing the magnifying glass into his back pocket.

When Alexa stood up and saw the mess of her tangled, wind-blown hair in the bathroom mirror, she exclaimed, "I second that!" She then began to rummage through the bathroom drawers looking for the perfect brush and styling spray to fix her unruly, strawberry-blond hair.

Rex let out a roaring "***Meow!***" bolting out the door with his tail between his legs, straight for his litter box.

"Well, you better come back when you're done and help clean up this mess, you pesky pet," Jake warned as he looked around the room at all the tossed bath towels and empty cardboard toilet paper rolls.

Alexa unzipped Sandy, and they all quickly got to work cleaning up the bathroom, minus Rex of course, who was otherwise occupied. "What are we going to do with all these empty toilet paper tubes, Jake?" she asked.

"I don't know, but we better hide them before Mom and Dad find out all the toilet paper is gone!"

Jake and Alexa, with Sandy scurrying closely behind, quickly gathered up all the unraveled cardboard tubes, then kicked, rolled, and pushed them all into Jake's room.

Sandy tried to shove a tube under Jake's bed with no luck.

"No, sweetie, that won't work," explained Alexa. "Jake's race car bed sits flat on the floor. You can't hide anything under there."

"Mmmmm—" he pondered. "Now let me think!"

Jake walked all around his room that was scattered with stacks and stacks of books, trophies, and sweaty, old socks thrown all over the place, looking for a perfect hiding place.

"I got it!" he exclaimed. "I got it!"

"Where?" Alexa screeched. "Where?"

"The closet!"

"Oh, no!" cried out Alexa. "I'm not going in there. It's way too scary. Why, it's like another universe under all that hunka-junk! Plus, it's stinky in there!"

"That's my point!" he explained. "No one would ever dare go in there! It's the perfect hiding place!"

Reluctantly, Alexa and Sandy agreed. Jake opened up the double-hung, enormous, white doors and pushed his back up against all the clutter to hold everything back from falling out. One by one, the girls pushed, shoved, piled, and placed all the empty toilet paper rolls into the cluttered closet. As Jake held back the massive cardboard wall, Alexa and Sandy attempted to close the doors.

"Hey!" shouted out Jake, "I'm supposed to be on the outside, not the inside!"

"Sorry!" she laughed. Alexa and Sandy cracked the doors open just a little so Jake could squeeze through. Then all three gave it one good, strong push, shutting the door.

"There, all done!" announced Jake. "Mom and Dad will never know!"

Suddenly, the right closet door popped open from the force of the over-abundance of junk pushing on it. Alexa raised her left eyebrow and smirked, "Ya' sure about that!" pointing to the door.

Jake grumbled in frustration, trying to figure out a solution to his dilemma. Scanning the room, he spotted his lacrosse stick lying next to his bed and got an idea. He grabbed it, and propped it up against the closet door wedging it shut. "Now—that'll work!"

"What happens when you have a game?" Alexa asked.

"I'll worry about that later," he thought.

Alexa and Jake heard Grandma calling from the playroom. "Jake—you need to pick up your coin collection before your parents get back!"

"Coming, Grandma!" he yelled down as he hid Grandpa's leather bound book under the hood of his blue race car bed.

Jake slid down the long banister railing as Alexa scooped up Sandy and her Inspector Girl backpack and headed for her bedroom. She gave Sandy a sweet kiss on her head and placed her into her pink cage next to the big, bay window across from Alexa's white princess bed. Alexa then dug through her backpack for the two sheets of paper from Great-Great-Grandma Mary's letter and then hid them in her pants pocket. Knowing Grandma was in the playroom helping Jake pick up his coins, she scooted unnoticed down to the kitchen. She ever-so-quietly tip-toed into the room, where she found Rex licking up some leftover custard filling from his Critter Detective cat food dish.

"Shhhhh—" she signaled to Rex. "We need to find a spot to put the second sheet of the letter so Grandma will find it."

Letting out a quiet "*Meow*," Rex pointed his paw up to Grandma's recipe box still sitting on the granite counter top next to the tall pile of cream puffs.

"Oooo, good idea!" she whispered softly. "I'll place the second sheet in the back of the box. She'll definitely find it there! Go check on Grandma in the playroom. Let me know when she's coming this way!"

Rex ran down the long hallway, slipping and sliding on the highly polished wood floor towards the children's playroom. Grandma and Jake were just packing up the last of the loose coins that had been scattered around the floor.

"Oh— I forgot!" announced Jake as he started pulling all his pants pockets inside-out, searching for his Indian head penny. "**GOT IT!**"

"What's that?" asked Grandma curiously.

Jake handed her the coin as he explained where he had found it that morning at the school playground. "You know—" he said, "that's not an Indian's face on the coin. It's the designer of the coin, James Longacre's, daughter. And that Indian headdress she's wearing belonged to an Indian chief by the name of Buffalo Hump!"

"Wow!" exclaimed Grandma. "I didn't know that! You really are a smart one—just like your dad and your grandpa." Beneath her very thick glasses she got a sad look in her radiant, blue eyes and sighed, "How he loved collecting coins."

"I miss Grandpa," Jake said equally sad.

"I do, too, my darling," she stuttered, holding back her tears. "I do, too."

Rex came bolting into the room with that familiar, blue handkerchief still dangling from around his neck. Grandma, utterly surprised, adjusted her glasses on the tip of her nose to get a better look at the handkerchief.

"Wherever did Rex get your grandfather's handkerchief from?" she asked in a suspicious voice.

Jake was taken off guard, not knowing that the blue handkerchief Snodgrass was wearing actually belonged to his grandfather. With a very serious thinking face, he quickly tried to come up with an answer without revealing the truth. "Ummmm—" he stuttered. "I—I—found it in the— ummmm—attic! Yeah—the—attic."

A bewildered look came over Grandma's face. "Now, how did it get there?" she wondered. "I haven't seen that handkerchief since the day your grandpa went— off to—"

"Went off to what—Grandma?" questioned Jake.

Grandma, not wanting to answer Jake's question, became all flustered. "Oh, oh, never mind," she stuttered nervously as she went to pet Rex. "It's not that important, anyway." She looked down at Rex, gave him a big kiss on the head, and said, "You look very handsome in blue, my old friend."

Rex gave her a warm snuggle and let out a loving, **"*Meow!*"**

"Oh, dear, my cake!" she shrieked, remembering it was baking in the oven.

Grandma scurried quickly into the kitchen to check on her cake with Rex and Jake tagging along close behind.

"What's the matter, Grandma?" asked Alexa as she closed the lid on the recipe box.

"I forgot all about my cake in the oven," she explained with a worried look as she put on her favorite, red, lobster claw oven mitts. "I hope it hasn't burned."

Jake and Alexa stood on either side of the oven in anticipation of the sweet treat. Licking his lips expectantly, Rex jumped up onto a stool to get a better view of what was coming out of the oven. Grandma ever-so-carefully slid the cake out of the oven. The heavenly aroma filled the room as she flipped over her baking pan onto a cookie sheet to unveil the cake.

"I got this recipe off the Internet!" she explained. "I've just been dying to try it out. Isn't it a beautiful *upside-down, downside-up, pineapple cake?* I hope it tastes as good as it looks." As she turned around, the children and Rex stood there speechless, frowning at her cake. "What's the matter? I thought you'd love this! You three look like you just saw a ghost."

Remembering Mrs. Smythe, with her poisoned lemon tarts and infamous upside-down, downside-up, pineapple cake, was still running around loose somewhere after escaping from prison, Jake stuttered, "It—it looks really good, Grandma."

"Yeah, Grandma," added Alexa, stuttering herself, in fear as she glared at the mounds of pineapples dripping off

the cake. "Real good—but I think—I'll have some—cream puffs for dessert instead. Cream puffs—definitely, cream puffs."

"Me, too!" exclaimed Jake.

"Well, maybe Rex would like to have a big juicy piece."

"*Meow, meow!*" he cried out in distaste.

Grandma flipped through her recipe box to find the cake recipe mumbling, "It's just a cake. It won't kill you!"

"I wouldn't be too sure about that," Jake whispered to Alexa and Rex.

"Yeah," whispered back Alexa. "You can't always trust what you get off the Internet these days. It could be a poisonous recipe!"

"*Meow!*" agreed Rex.

Suddenly, Grandma let out a startled cry as she leafed through her recipe box. "Where in the world did this come from?"

"What, Grandma?" the children shouted.

"I just don't believe it. Why it's the second half of Great-Great-Grandma Mary's letter. I have looked through this box a hundred times. Now, why didn't I ever notice that there before? I must need thicker glasses!"

"I don't think they make 'em any thicker than that, Grandma!" Jake snickered.

Glaring at him as her glasses slipped down to the tip of her nose, she stated, "Not only do you have your grandfather's brains, you also have his amusing and somewhat annoying sense of humor, I see!"

"Sorry, but they are a little thick!" he said, somewhat apologetically.

Grandma giggled as she tousled Jake's hair. "Very

funny! Grandmas are supposed to have thick glasses. It's a sign of years of wisdom!"

"Now you can add the molasses to your barbeque sauce to make it just right!" blurted out Alexa.

Jake and Rex gave her the most unbelievable look for shouting that out before Grandma actually read the letter.

Grandma then read the missing ingredient from the letter, "*Molasses!*" she exclaimed. "Now—how did you know that?"

"Lucky guess????" mumbled Jake.

"Yeah," stuttered Alexa while her eyes roamed the room. "A— a—lucky guess!"

The children breathed a sigh of relief when Mom and Dad, interrupting the moment, came storming into the kitchen with bags and bags of groceries for the barbeque.

"The strangest thing happened at the food store," Mom said. "When we arrived, there wasn't a drop of milk to be found anywhere. Then, all of a sudden, while we were checking out, the shelves were being stocked left and right with white, chocolate, and, of course, Alexa's favorite milk, strawberry!"

"How weird is that?" exclaimed Dad.

Jake and Alexa giggled their way out of the kitchen as they ran to help with the packages. Rex shot out the door right behind them.

"Lexy, I can't believe you shouted out 'molasses' before Grandma read the letter," Jake scolded, grabbing a case of soda from the trunk of Dad's car.

"*Meow!*" grumbled Rex in agreement.

"Sorry, it just blurted out!" Alexa said. "I'm sure our

secret's safe. It's not like Grandma has any idea where we've been or what we've been up to!"

"You're probably right," agreed Jake, "but we have to be more careful in the future. If anyone finds out about the magnifying glass's secret, their lives could be in— *DANGER!*"

They all agreed, dragging the rest of the groceries into the house. The kitchen was in such a buzz of chaos and excitement as everyone prepared for the arrival of the Moustachio's guests. Alexa frantically searched the bags for any signs of the Clunky Chunky Chocolate Bars, while Rex started his own search, jumping into a bag of his own.

"Any luck?" she asked.

"*Meow!*" Rex purred in satisfaction as he dragged out a big bag of Clunky Chunkys.

"*Lexy,*" Dad said in his firm voice. "You're not planning on giving Rex a Clunky Chunky, are you?"

"Well, I did promise him, Daddy!"

Rex just stood there with his big, golden eyes pathetically begging Dad's permission while the bag of Clunky Chunkys was firmly gripped between his teeth, dangling back and forth.

"Please, Daddy?"

"Oh, all right," Dad agreed reluctantly as he dug through one of the shopping bags for himself, "but remember, just one!"

"Thank you, Daddy!"

"Here it is!" exclaimed Dad, pulling out a huge bottle of barbeque sauce with an enormous smile on his face.

"What in heaven's name is that?" chuckled Grandma.

Mom opened up the refrigerator to reveal ten unfinished

bottles of Dad's barbeque sauces. She declared to Grandma with a frustrated look on her face, "You know how your son loves to collect his barbeque sauces. Just look at this refrigerator. His collection grows bigger every week!"

"This new sauce is going to help me make the best spareribs ever!" he announced, holding up the massive bottle with hope. Dad read the label out loud, "***BIG DADDY'S BARBEQUE SAUCE, THE BIGGEST BARBEQUE SAUCE THERE EVER WAS AND WILL EVER BE.*** You know, it has molasses in it!"

"***Really,***" Grandma said curiously as she read the ingredients then turned to stare at the children suspiciously.

Dad ran upstairs to wash up and grab his favorite barbeque apron with the black and white cow patches on it. In the meantime, everyone folded up the shopping bags and put away the last of the groceries.

"Honey," Dad yelled down to Mom in a questioning voice. "Are we out of toilet paper?"

"In the kid's bathroom," she yelled up.

"No, there's not," he yelled back down.

The children kept busy with the groceries, trying not to show their guilt.

Mom became annoyed, knowing Dad could never find anything by himself. As she made her way upstairs to help, she called out, "You just bought a truck load the other day. It couldn't have just disappeared into thin air!"

Mom searched all the bathrooms for the missing toilet paper, while Dad checked out the hall closets. While passing Jake's room, he noticed the lacrosse stick propped up against the closet doors. "Now how many times have I told him that stick can bend if you shove it against a door," Dad thought. The moment he went to remove the stick, Jake's closet doors flew open, burying Dad, head to toe, in all those empty cardboard toilet paper tubes.

"*Jake!*" he exploded.

"I think now might be a good time for you three to scoot outside and play in the backyard before your friends arrive," shushed Grandma.

"Good idea!" agreed the children fearfully, as they bolted out the backdoor. "Good idea!"

Jake and Alexa ran out into the bright sunlight beaming over the Moustachio's beautiful backyard. They ran around the massive, perfectly groomed, deep-green lawn. The area was framed with an array of brightly colored flowers that Mom meticulously attended.

Rex scooted behind as the children jumped up onto the swings dangling from their play yard. They swung back and forth high into the sky as Rex darted up the ladder on the redwood tree fort covered by a hunter-green canvas roof. He slid down the matching green slide while making a silly spectacle of himself.

"Well—that was quite a mystery we solved, wasn't it Inspector Girl?" Jake declared, giving his sister a mid-air high-five.

"Most definitely, Inspector!" she agreed with a warm smile. "Most definitely! So—where do you think Mrs. Smythe and Snodgrass are hiding out?"

"I don't know," he thought. "But one thing's for sure—"

"What's that?"

"We haven't seen the last of them!"

"*Meow!*" agreed Rex, shooting down the slide again.

"*Meow!*"

Suddenly, they heard a car pull up in the driveway. Recognizing the fancy white car with the shiny wheels, Alexa shouted, "Oooo—that's Grace." She jumped off the swing and ran quickly towards the driveway. "Come on, Jake, we're going to get a game of House Detective started once everyone else arrives!"

Jake jumped off the swing and followed Rex up the back steps of the fort. "I'll be there in a minute!" he yelled out. Jake sat at the edge of the slide with Rex curled up on his lap. Unexpectedly, he heard a squawking sound in the sky. He looked up, but for a moment the brightness of the sun blinded his view as a dark shadow flew over his head. Suddenly, Jake felt a clunk on his head as something fell from the sky. At the bottom of the slide, he found the fallen object. To his astonishment, it was one of the gold coins with Chief Buffalo Hump's face on it. He grabbed the coin and examined every inch of it with his magnifying glass. Its brilliant shine bounced off the face of the magnifying glass with every turn of Jake's wrist.

A wide smile spread across his face. Jake's dimples deepened as he looked up into the sky. He thought to himself about his grandpa, Big Daddy, the Comanche Indians, and his fateful battle with Snodgrass. He thought about the crazy world he'd gotten to see, and he went off to play, thinking of the many misadventures that were yet to be!

THE END?

Now Read Book Three!

THE CURSE OF SHIPWRECK BOTTOM

Brave, young Jake Moustachio is quickly learning to control the powers of his magical magnifying glass, and not a moment too soon!

The destiny of our young sleuth and his companions starts to become apparent as they are tossed into a double-crossing, fantastic world on the high seas. Earth's End awaits our unsuspecting hero, his sister, Alexa, and their crime solving pets as they navigate an ocean full of the most treacherous suspects, sailing about on the other side of his grandpa's mystical magnifying glass. Captain Snappy, a cranky pirate, calls upon Jake to break a curse cast upon his ship and crew by the wicked sea witch, Jezebel.

Also sailing among the tumultuous waves of the sea is the evil Baron Von Snodgrass and his unrecognizable evil partner, who is more determined than ever to stop the young Moustachio and snatch his magnifying glass. There is only one guy who can solve the puzzle to reverse the curse and save the world from its impending destruction. Inspector Moustachio is his name, and solving mysteries is his specialty.

Join Inspector Jake Moustachio, his sister, Alexa (a.k.a. Inspector Girl), her precious pet guinea pig, Sandy, and their crazy cat, Rex, in their next swashbuckling misadventure...

IF YOU ENJOYED

THE MYSTERY AT COMANCHE CANYON

BE SURE TO READ

BOOK ONE
The Case of Stolen Time
ISBN 9780979087899

BOOK THREE
The Curse of Shipwreck Bottom
ISBN 9780979757228

AND DISCOVER THE REST OF THE MISADVENTURES!

Look for
The Misadventures of Inspector Moustachio
series at your local bookstores and libraries, or order online.

Published By

Community PRESS

239 Windbrooke Lane, Virginia Beach VA 23462

About The Author...

Wayne Madsen is a dad from New Jersey. In 2007, he was nationally recognized as a **Reading is Fundamental (RIF)** booklist pick author for the first book in *The Misadventures of Inspector Moustachio* series.

Book one, **The Case of Stolen Time**, book two, **The Mystery of Comanche Canyon**, and book three, **The Curse of Shipwreck Bottom**, have become must-reads on school and library reading lists.

The Misadventures of Inspector Moustachio series is also a celebrated winner of the distinguished **iParenting Media Award**, a Disney Interactive Group Media Property.

Wayne's inspiration for writing comes from the real-life antics and misadventures of his children, Jake and Alexa. Adding in the escapades of the Madsen's crazy pets, Wayne has created an amazing universe of unforgettable characters who have become favorites on family bookshelves everywhere.

Wayne has just completed the fourth book in *The Misadventures of Inspector Moustachio* series, **The Secret of the Pharaoh's Feline**. He is currently working on book five, **The Mishap with the Mad Scientist**.

Read What They Are Saying About
The Misadventures of
Inspector Moustachio!

What a recipe for success! Madsen took a handful of magic, added it to a bucket of adventure, threw in a scoop of history, and wound it all around two believable kids to create *The Mystery at Comanche Canyon*.

The intrepid young detectives, Alexa & Jake, gain confidence in this new tale. This is a great read for parents to share with their children. It is full of humor and excitement for adults and children alike. The readers happily follow the two young sleuths—and their animal companions—as they learn more about the powers of the mysterious magnifying glass and their dangerous nemesis, the evil Baron Von Snodgrass. I hope their escapades continue!

Chris Moore
Director of Education
Sylvan Learning Center

The Mystery at Comanche Canyon is an excellent follow up to *The Case of Stolen Time*. Once again we are brought into the wonderful world of Inspector Moustachio, where Jake, Lexy, and of coarse Rex, take us on a delightful journey to solve yet another mystery. This book is filled with action, adventure, comedy and a group of lovable characters to make any child smile. It's a great book for every boy and girl, no matter how old or young! The author truly knows how to make his audience want more misadventures—book after book!

Janine Bubet
Children's Department Manager
Barnes & Noble

A happy book with interesting twists and turns. Its images come alive with adventure and suspense. The characters wit and humor bring the story to life. Refreshing and lots of fun!

Mary Mandel
Lead Children's Bookseller
Barnes & Noble

CPSIA information can be obtained at www.ICGtesting.com
Printed in the USA
BVOW070555121011

273437BV00003B/42/P